BLACKBONE:
THE REUNION

BY: CARYN LEE

BLACKBONE: THE REUNION

- Written by -

CARYN LEE

Copyright © 2016 by Caryn Lee

Published by Caryn Lee

Fifth Edition

Facebook: https://www.facebook.com/caryndeniselee?fref=ts

Cover design/Graphics: Angel Walker

Chapter One

Ring…..Ring…..Ring…… Who in the hell is calling my house phone at three am in the morning. The only people who had my house number were family. I reached for the cordless phone knocking it on the floor. It continued ring as I picked it up, seeing the 630 area code made me nervous. That only meant one thing, that it was a call from Chicago. I answered it quickly.

"Hello."

"Hello may I speak with Ciara.

"This is she, who is this? What's going on?" I asked nervously. By now Kanye was awake, rubbing my shoulders.

"This is Nurse Fuller from Edwards Hospital." I became short of breath grabbing my chest, as she continued to talk. "I'm calling to inform you that your mother is in the hospital. She was found unconscious in her home by her neighbor and was brought here by ambulance.

"Oh my God is she fine?" Tears started falling down my face as I was prepared to hear the worse.

"Yes she's stable now. The paramedic took your number off her refrigerator and provided it to us. Do you have time to talk about your mother condition?"

"Yes I can talk right now."

Nurse Fuller and I talked for twenty minutes. She explained to me that my mother had Cirrhosis of the liver and Hepatitis C. All of this was too hard for me to take in right now. I was not understanding how she occurred Cirrhosis when my mother haven't had a drink in years. Nurse Fuller bust my bubble when she told me that in fact my mother had alcohol in her system when she arrived to the hospital. I was so upset and furious when I found out that my mother had started drinking again. All this time she has been lying to me, Brenda was back to her old self again.

"What's going on Ciara? Is everything okay with your mother?" Kanye asked me.

"No, she's not doing too well." I began to cry uncontrollably. Kanye wrapped held me in his arms. "I have to go to Chicago immediately to see about my mother."

"Do whatever it is that you need to do baby."

Kanye rocked me in his arms as I cried. The last thing that I wanted to do was go back to Chicago right now. Damn, my family and I had our summer already planned and was looking forward to Disney World. I only had one mother, by me being her only child I had to step up.

In the morning when Eric Jr. and Kenya woke up Kanye and I had to tell them news. After the phone call we didn't go back to sleep. We spent the time booking flights and packing. I purchased four one way tickets to Chicago for me and the children. I didn't have any idea how long that I was going to be in Chicago that's why I didn't purchase round trip tickets. Kanye couldn't be with me at the time

2

because he was working on a major contract. Besides this was my mother and my problem that I had to deal with and he understood that. I promised him that I would facetime him and call as much as possible. When we told the children that they had to go to Chicago, by surprise they weren't mad at all. In fact Eric Jr. was happy to visit because he wanted to see his father. I haven't or Eric Jr. have seen Smooth in three years, but once a year I would fly to Chicago to check on my boutique without Smooth knowing. Three years ago Smooth and Erica flew to Arizona to see his son and her little brother, things didn't go to well. Instead of focusing on his child, Smooth was trying to establish another relationship with me. Kanye wasn't haven't that bullshit and things got physical. Both of them had a fight in front of the children and Smooth was arrested. I was so embarrassed, after that I cut Smooth ignorant ass off from his child. Smooth threaten to take me to court but he didn't. Smooth knew better than to fuck with me. Over time I got over it and allowed Smooth to talk and see his son on his IPhone that he provided for him. I was over with Smooth and his hood ways. You would think that he has grown up after so many years being that he was older than me. Needless to say that the children were excited and couldn't wait to get to Chicago.

We landed safely arriving at seven pm Chicago time. Eric Jr and Kenya were hungry and crabby and so was I. We picked up our luggage and stepped outside.

"Hey sister over here!" I heard a familiar squeaky voice yell.

I looked over to my right, Kelly short ass was standing next to her truck. "Auntie Kelly!" Eric Jr. yelled as he ran to her. "I miss my babies so much, look at how big you have gotten." Kelly gave him a big hug.

I walked over with Kenya, she was more reserved and was acting shy. Which I don't know why because she met Kelly before. Over the years Kelly and her children have been to see me twice in Arizona. I looked inside the truck and didn't see her children.

"Hey sis, how are you? Where are the children?" I asked her as we hugged.

"I left their bad asses at home with their father." Kelly laughed.

We placed our luggage into the trunk and jumped into her Range Rover. "Please take us to Portillo's, we are starving."

Kelly pulled off, it feel weird being home. So much has changed since the last time that I was here. After the restaurant Kelly dropped me and the children off at my mother home. Three years ago I went through Kelly's real estate company to purchase my mother home. Kelly managed to find a three bedroom for two hundred thousand dollars. With the help and the connections of my hardworking husband, he managed to have the renovations done for only another fifty thousand. My mother didn't have to worry about paying her mortgage because I paid it every month. My boutiques were doing excellent and have grown across the map. Bella Boutiques were now in Arizona, Atlanta, Texas and Chicago. I'm currently working on trying to open one in Los Angles but it's extremely hard to make happen. As the children and I stepped inside I can see that my mother has a good job at keeping the place together. Her furniture looked as if no one has ever sat on it. The children and I sat at the kitchen table eating our beefs. I tried to maintain a straight face but inside I was worried about my mother. After we ate I Face Time called Kanye to let him know that we arrived to Chicago safely.

"Hello husband the children and I are here at my mother place."

"That's good to know that you are. I miss you all so much already Ciara."

"I miss you as well. I really wish that you could be here with us."

"As soon I get a chance I promise to fly there as soon as I can."

I continued the conversation and passed the phone to the children. After talking for a while I started to yarn. Kanye seen that I was tired ending the conversation. I had to get the children to bed because they were tired as well. I took my mother room, Kenya was in one room, while Eric Jr. was in the other room. I made sure that they were in their pajamas and off to bed. We had a very long day tomorrow and all had to be up in the morning to see about my mother.

The next day I woke up, everyone got dressed and we were out the door by nine am. My mother didn't have any food so I was going to feed them something off the dollar menu from McDonalds. That would just have to do until I make it to the grocery store. It didn't take long to make it to Edwards Hospital. When we arrived Brenda was lying in bed watching television.

"Hey Ma! How are you doing?" Brenda jumped up and was surprised to see us.

"Ciara, what are you doing here?"

"I'm here to check on you." I gave my mother a hug as well as the kids.

"Oh my grand babies are here to. I miss you all, come and sit by me."

They sat on the side of the bed next to their grandmother. I looked at my mother, it was almost as if I didn't recognize her. She lost weight everywhere but in her abdomen. Her stomach was huge like she was six months pregnant and she had a bad case of jaundice. I don't know if I should be sad or upset about this situation. Brenda noticed the look on my face but ignored it as she continued to be entertained by her grandchildren. An hour into the visit the doctor arrived and explained that Brenda will be having surgery tomorrow first thing in the morning. It was time for us all to eat because the children were getting hungry.

"Ma I'll be back in an hour. The children and I are going to the cafeteria to grab something to eat." I kissed her on the forehead.

"Take your time sugar. I'm going to get some sleep. All the medicine that I'm taking is making me feel drowsy." She rolled over, pulling the cover over her shoulder.

I took the children downstairs to eat after we were finished and made it back to the room, Brenda was sleeping. Instead of going inside the children and I left. Besides we had to go grocery shopping to buy some food for the house. While I grocery shopped I talked to my husband to tell him how my day was going so far. Throughout the day I spoke to London and a few other people that I had to connect with informing them that I was back home. I didn't bother to go back up to the hospital till the morning.

Kelly was at my mother's house bright and early in the morning. She was here to come get the children so that I could be by my mother's side at the hospital.

"Thank you so much for during this favor for me Kelly."

"Sis you don't have to thank me. Go up there and handle your business. The children and I are going to the zoo. I have a fun day planned for them. Oh by the way, Ant told Smooth that you were in town. I'm just giving you a heads up so don't be surprised if he will be contacting you soon." Kelly chuckled.

I laughed and thought about Smooth for a moment. It has been a very long time since I've seen him. I know that he may have some built up anger about me inside of him. When I get to that bridge then I will cross it. Till then I had to be worried about my mother and not my crazy children's father. It was five am when I made it to the hospital. Surgery was scheduled for six am. My mother was awake when I walked through her room door. She was wearing glasses and reading her bible. She looked up at me when she realized that I was in her room.

"I didn't mean to disturb you. I'll just sit here quietly until you're done reading." I was preparing to take a sit in the small chair in the corner.

"No Ciara please come closer." I walked over to my mother and burst into tears. I could no longer hold them inside any longer. She held me in her arms, "Baby girl I'm sorry about letting you down. I know that it's very hard for you to see me like this."

"Why did you have to start back drinking again? You were doing fine after so many years." I wanted to know, I needed answers.

"After the break up with my man and with you not being here I became very depressed. It was easier for me to pick up a drink. Overtime the drink helped ease the pain."

"No it was easier for you to pick up the phone and to call me. You know what's crazy, deep down inside I felt that something weird was going on. We used to facetime all the time, when you stop accepting my facetime calls it was because you didn't want me to see how you were looking. I begged you to move to Arizona with me, but you didn't want to come. I didn't want or never intended on leaving you alone. I was always a phone call and flight away."

The transporters knocked on the door interrupting our private conversation. They were ready to take her off to have surgery. They stepped inside, asked my mother her name, she responded and then they took a look at her identification bracelet. Before she left I gave her a hug and a kiss.

"I love you mom." I held her hand and didn't want to let go.

"Please forgive me, I love you so much Ciara. Tell my grand babies that I love them too."

They wheeled her off to surgery which was going to take two hours. I sat around and waited inside her room occupying myself with a few of my business projects that I was working on. I brought my MacBook Pro with me and used the hospital Wi-Fi. I called Kelly to check on her and the children, they were having so much fun that they didn't have time to talk to me. Kanye face time called me on the other line so I had to end the call with my best friend. Seeing Kanye face brought a smile on my face. I applied more lip gloss on my lips so that they could be popping when I talked to my husband.

"Give me a kiss beautiful, I miss you so damn much."
Kanye said.

I blew my hubby several kisses. Kanye looked so damn
handsome with his hard hat on. He was out on the field
working on a very important project. I could see and hear
the machines in the background. Kanye walked off to a
quieter and secluded area so that we could both hear one
another. Once he was ready to talk he gave me his
undivided attention. His facial expression went from happy
to serious.

"Is everything fine Ciara? I could tell by your eyes that
you've been crying baby."

"Yes I was crying before my mom went to surgery.
Everything is fine, I'm okay. How is your day going?" I
changed the subject off of me and made it about him. I
didn't want my husband to be worried about me. He needed
to focus one hundred percent on the major project that he
was working on.

We were able to talk to one another for thirty minutes until
he went back to work. Deep down inside I wished that
Kanye was with me right now. The time went by very
quickly as I sat there waiting. The nurse and doctor came

walking into my mother's room with an uneasy look upon her face.

"Excuse me Mrs. I regret to inform you that your mother had some complications during surgery and she passed away. She developed a blot clot that traveled to her lungs, blocking her blood flow. We tried our best to stop the pulmonary embolism but we couldn't. We will give you a moment to be with her alone and we deeply apologize."

"What are you saying?! Please tell me that you are lying?! You're lying right?! This can't be happening right now!" I grabbed the doctor by his collar, yelling in his face. The nurse tried to pull us apart but she wasn't strong enough. I smacked the nurse across her face before security came rushing into the room separating me from everyone. They carried my tiny frame away to the corner of the room. While the doctor and nurse exited the room.

"They killed my mother!" I wept and sobbed. It took security an hour to calm me down inside that room.

Chapter Two

I was busy taking care of business when Ant hit me up and told me the good news. Hearing that my baby Ciara was in town was the highlight of my day. I didn't have a number on her, but I did know that she was staying at her mother's place. I heard that Brenda was in the hospital and that was the reason why she was in town. While sitting at my desk, I realized that I finally had the chance to see Eric Jr. Due to my absurd behavior, Ciara didn't allow me near my son. Over the years my mother and I have only seen Junior through face time calls. My mother tried to talk to Ciara so that she could change her mind, but Ciara wasn't going for that. That was the past and I'm no longer that person. I've matured, grown up and accepted the mistakes and bad choices that I made in my past. Speaking of which, here comes one bad choice that I made right now.

Kayla swayed her hips as she walked through my office door carrying the shopping bags of clothes for Erica. Before she sat down she had a slay look upon her face. Bracing myself for whatever she was about to say, I popped two Advil's for the migraine that she was about to give me.

"Here are the clothes that I bought and picked out for Erica. Smooth I need a big favor? I came up with a new idea and business that I want to start. I was thinking about starting a swimwear line."

Kayla was always begging and shit. "Why are you coming to me Kayla?"

"The problem is that I don't have the money to get started. I need at least fifty thousand to get everything on the roll. Can I please have the money? I promise that I would give you every penny back."

"No. You're trying to do too much Kayla. I gave you the money to open up that damn shoe store, you better focus on that before you plan on starting something new."

"My shoe boutique isn't doing that good in sales."

"Maybe because you're not focusing on your business. Instead you're too busy partying and running the streets. You barely have Variyah, you're prancing around in these streets like you don't have any responsibilities."

"Look I'm a boss bitch and I have a reputation to live by. The streets is the only way that I know how to get money. Smooth that was a low blow for you to bring up our daughter."

"It's true Kayla, my mother always have her. As a matter of fact she's raised her since she's born. You were released, you went back in and of course she had her again. Kayla it's time for you to grow up and be a mother to your daughter, before these streets take you down."

"You know what Smooth this is both of our child. Ever since the beginning you have put her off on me as if you didn't create her. I let you have me whenever you want and do whatever you ask me to do, now I can't get any help?! You aren't shit Smooth!"

"Kayla you know what your problem is? Your problem is that you're always playing the fucking victim. Get out of my face, you're wasting my time sitting here begging me for something that you won't get out of me. Go to your store and run your business."

Kayla got up and stormed out of my office slamming the door behind her. How dare she bring that negative energy into my place of business? I was at my Landscaping Company going over some paperwork. Business was doing great being that it was the season for lawn work. I had money to make but more importantly Ciara and Eric Jr was my priority.

The day went by fast as I handled business making sure that everything was flowing. When I looked up it was four pm and time for me to start heading to my mother's house. My mother called and asked me to stop by her home so that she could talk with me. Pulling up to my mother's house was such a beautiful sight. All of my hard work in the streets had paid off allowing me to purchase my mother a bigger home. She moved from Bellwood to Oswego in a four bedroom, 97 square feet single family home. When I was younger I promised to take care of my mother for as long as she lived. As I pulled into the driveway Erica and Variyah were waiting for me at the door. They put a smile on my face, brighten my day and made me forget all about the bullshit that I dealt with today. Erica sprinted off toward me leaving Variyah standing at the door as I got out of my drop top Maserati grabbing the bags out of the backseat.

"Daddy what did you bring me?" She was excited to see me.

"I have Chinese food and summer clothes for my precious daughter. Where is your grandmother?"

"Grandma is in the house." Erica gave me a big hug, after that she took the bags from me sprinting off into the house.

She was excited to see what she had as she went through the clothing pulling out piece by piece. "Daddy when will I be able to pick out my own clothes?" Her face grew from a smile to a frown. That indicated that she didn't like the clothes that Kayla picked out for her.

"What's wrong with your face?" Tilting Erica head back as I stared in her eyes that are very similar to mine."

"Daddy I don't like any of these clothes. They are all childish and not my type. Daddy I am eleven years old now. Why can't I pick out my own clothes?" Erica whined to me.

That was a difficult decision for me to make. My baby girl and first born was growing up right before my eyes. She was a spitting image of me, but had her mother's Rochelle genes, her curves and bossy way. I could see that I was going to have to lay my hands on some boys in the future. My mother joined us in the dining room. Promising Erica that I would think about it, I ended the conversation peacefully. I stood up to give my mother a huge hug.

"How are you doing mom? The beef and broccoli and the rest of the Chinese food is in the bags on the table." I went to the bathroom to wash my hands. My mother was making the plates of food for everyone. We all took a seat, said grace and started eating. Both Erica and Variyah had to be hungry because they stuffed their mouth with shrimp fried rice. Shaking my head I laughed at them both before my mother started to speak.

"I take it that you haven't heard the news about Ciara?" She asked.

"Yes I heard that Ciara and Eric Jr. was here in town."

"Smooth yes they are, but it more to that. Ciara called me today and told me that her mother passed away. Apparently Brenda was sick and died during surgery. Ciara was very distraught that I didn't get a chance to speak to Jr. I think that you should give her a call to see how she's doing."

Damn I sat there speechless as my heart dropped for Ciara. This was not the news that I was expecting to hear. Suddenly my appetite disappeared and I wanted to run to Ciara need.

"Excuse me mom, I need to make a phone call."

"Handle your business son, her number is sitting on my bible in the living room." My mother nodded her head as if she was one of my friends telling me to go handle my business.

She and my daughters continued to eat their Chinese food as I stepped away from the dining room for some privacy. I dialed the number that was on the piece of paper. The phone rang about three times before her voicemail came on. I didn't bother to leave a voicemail, I had another plan on my mind. Going back into the dining room, I continued to eat with my mother and daughters before I left. An hour later I made sure that my daughters were in bed and that my mother was straight. My mom knew what was on my mind. She gave me a kiss on the forehead and looked into my eyes.

"Don't go over there acting a fool. Ciara needs you as friend right now, leave all that mess from the past behind you." She took a seat in her favorite chair, opened up her bible and started reading it.

Taking her advice, I left out heading toward Naperville. On the way there I called Ant to tell him my next move. Don't nobody know how much love Ciara has for me, more than Ant and Kelly does. Ant picked up on the second ring.

"Yo, what's up my nigga? Ant hit his blunt letting out a few coughs.

"Man I'm on my way to Ciara's mom house. Did you hear about Brenda passing away?"

"Kelly just told me an hour ago. I hit your line but you didn't answer. That's fucked up what happened." Ant exhaled.

"Yes that is, I just left from my mom house. She just told me everything that happened. I decided to go by to send my condolences."

"Smooth be easy, you know what happened the last time when you and Ciara saw one another."

"I'm not on no more bullshit. I got this, besides Ciara needs all the support that she could get."

"Good copy, Kelly and the kids are over there right now with her. As a matter of fact, let me get my ass up and meet you over there. Aye did you holler at dude yet from North Caroline about that?" Ant coughed again.

We changed the subject from personal to business. As I drove on the highway I hollered at Ant about a few things that were about to go down. We were all about to make some major moves soon in the Chicago if everything went as planned. I've been trying to catch up with Red, that nigga was always back and forth out of town. Vell was prepared and down for whatever. At the speed that I was driving, 70 miles per hour. I managed to arrive to

Naperville in about thirty minutes without getting pulled over by the state troopers. Upon pulling up Kelly's Range was parked in the driveway. I parked my whipped in front of Brenda's home. Shit I'm not going to lie I was nervous about seeing Ciara because of our last encounter. This could either go right or left, I was praying that it went right. My fingers pressed on the doorbell heavily. I could hear voices, seconds later Kelly answered the door.

"Smooth, I'm surprised to see you." Kelly grabbed her chest smiling slightly.

"My mother told me what happened so I wanted to check on her."

Kelly stared at me, "Well you know that I have to check with my friend first before I let you in." She walked off leaving the door cracked just enough for me to hear. The children were playing so loudly that I could barely hear the conversation between Kelly and Ciara. Moments later Eric Junior ran to the door opening it with the other children behind him.

"Daddy! Daddy!" With a huge smile on his face, he hugged me.

Tears fell from my eyes as I picked him up, holding him tight. "I miss you so much son."

Kelly opened up the door allowing me to step inside. All of the children gathered around me, happy to see me as well and asking for money. Kelly and Ant twins, Jasmine and Justin; my god children were happy to see me too. One by one I gave them each a hug and some money.

"Thank you Uncle Smooth!" The twins ran off to play.

Eric Junior was still on my hip as I stood in the living room. Ciara appeared from the back holding her daughter Kenya's hand. We both locked eyes, hers were puffy and swollen from all the crying that she done. My heart started beating fast, as if I was on trial for murder. A million things went through my mind as I stared at the woman that I was in love with.

"Okay this is kind of weird. Are you two just going to stand there and stare at one another or are you going to say something?" Kelly burst out saying.

At that moment I walked up to Ciara and gave my baby a hug. She embraced me as her daughter Kenya tugged on her arm to stop.

"It's okay Kenya, he's only giving your momma a hug." Ciara said to her daughter.

Kenya was a resemblance of Ciara, dark and beautiful. "Hello Kenya, nice to meet you." I gave her my hand to hold. Kenya looked at her mom first before accepting my hand. Ciara nodded her head indicating to her that it was fine to accept my hand.

Eric Junior blurted out, "This is my daddy Kenya."

Everyone in the room laughed at his outburst. I put Eric Junior down for a minute and Ciara told him and Kenya to play with the twins. We stood face to face in front of one another. Tears trickled down her cheeks. I hugged her tightly, "It's okay to cry baby. I know how much you loved her." I continued to hold her until she released herself from my embrace.

"Smooth they killed my mother. Those assholes killed her!" Ciara cried.

"Baby everything will be fine. I will pay for the best lawyer and we will sue the doctors. Right now you have to calm down and mourn her loss. We all will make sure that Brenda is laid to rest properly." I looked over at Kelly letting her know that we got this. Seconds later the doorbell rang, that had to be Ant. Kelly stepped away to open the door as Ciara and I took a seat on the couch. Ant stepped inside, gave Kelly a hug and walked over to hug Ciara and give his condolences. We all were back together like when were younger. It felt good to be back around Ciara and my true people that I fucked with. Ciara went from crying to laughing as we all talked about the good old days.

Two hours later Kelly, Ant and the twins left to go home. Ciara and I were alone with Eric Junior and Kenya. Eric Junior was asleep on my lap. It has been a very long time since I've saw him. When it was time for me to put him to bed he didn't want me to go. I looked at Ciara as she carried Kenya to bed. I promised Eric Junior that I wasn't go anywhere.

"Smooth you know that you can't spend the night. Why would you lie to him?" Ciara said.

"I didn't lie, I'm not going anywhere."

Taking Ciara by surprise I kissed her, grabbing her ass and lifting her up. She didn't stop me from carrying her into Brenda's bedroom. We both kissed each other as we undressed. Ciara body was still beautiful, her dark skin was smooth and soft. I kissed her cut on her lower belly where they had to cut for my son's cesarean. That was a special

24

moment that we both shared in our lives. I continued to kiss and lick lower as I worked my way down between her legs.

"Smooth we can't do this. I'm married to Kanye, this isn't right." Ciara mouth said no but her eyes said yes.

"Fuck Kanye, you're my woman now."

Parting her thick thighs, I buried my face deep into her pussy. Ciara arched her back, pushing my head deeper into my pussy.

"Oh! Oh! Shit! Damn Smooth!" Ciara moaned in pleasure.

Turning her over, I kissed and licked all over her big, chocolate ass. Ciara jiggled her ass in face as I opened up her butt cheeks licking her asshole. She tooted her ass up allowing me to eat her ass.

"Smooth you're so fucking nasty. That shit feels so fucking good!"

My tongue fucked her ass as it smothered my face. Ciara was special so she got special treatment because I don't eat ass period, but she was an exception. Ciara moans made my dick harder, I couldn't wait any longer to feel the inside of her.

"Wait Smooth you have to put on a condom. I don't know who you've been fucking." Ciara stopped me.

Not wanting to argue. I went inside my pants pocket and took out a condom. I respected Ciara, hell I was blessed to even be in this situation right now. Anxiously I placed the rubber on my dick as Ciara watched me.

"What you don't trust me baby?" I laughed.

"Hell no I do not trust you. You good for sliding in my pussy raw just like the old times." Ciara giggled.

When I stuffed my dick inside her wet tight pussy. Her giggles changed to gasps, it's been a very long time since I've had my pussy. Stroking and pumping slowly. I took my time in this pussy, Ciara had a bomb. It was so hard for me not to bust fast because her pussy was so good. Fuck it, I had to go hard in this pussy and make up for all the years that I missed. I went deeper inside of her as Ciara threw her juicy ass back on my dick.

"Yes Smooth fuck me like you miss me. Ohhhhh yes!"

"I miss my pussy babe! I miss my sweet, tight pussy so much." I pumped faster.

"Yes please don't stop! Its right there baby! Ohhhhh I miss you so much!" Ciara moaned.

"You miss daddy?! Whose pussy is this?" I pumped faster, smacking Ciara on her ass. "Is this my pussy?"

"Yesssssss! Oh yes!" Ciara buckled under me as I bust my nut.

We both collapsed on the bed breathing heavily. I held Ciara in my arms as both of our phones rang. We both ignored the rings, enjoying one another presence. I wasn't going to allow nothing to stop this moment. It's been so damn long that I never wanted to let her go. We drifted off to sleep with my dick still inside of her.

Chapter Three

The sound of Smooth's voice woke me. I jumped up out of a deep sleep, it was 10:45 pm. Fuck! How did I managed to sleep so long? I was naked and could still smell Smooth's cologne on my body. My phone rang causing me to jump scaring the hell out of me. When I saw Kanye's picture and name pop up on my phone screen my heart starting pounding. I panicked as I answered my husband's face time call. Kanye's face popped onto the screen as I ran my fingers through my hair trying to smooth it out.

"Good morning sleepy head. I've been calling you all day and night. How are you doing today?" Kanye looked at me with concerned look on his face.

"I'm so sorry babe that I missed your calls. I was very exhausted after having such a very long day yesterday. I'm doing a little better, but would be better if you were here." I had to sneak in that part. Even though I just fucked my ex, I still loved my husband.

"Baby I wish that I could be there with you. As soon as you get the day for the funeral let me know. I promise you that I would be there by your side. Where are the children at lovely?" Damn, I knew that he was going to ask about the children.

I had to think of a lie quickly. "They are downstairs with Kelly and her children. She stayed over to help me out." I smiled.

"Great, that was nice of Kelly. I tell you what, honey why don't you give me a call after you get yourself together. I have to get back out there on the field to make sure that everything is flowing. I love and miss you and the children beautiful."

"I love you more handsome." I blew him a several kisses before ended the call.

After I hung up my smile fading away. I felt so guilty for lying to my husband.

Clap! Clap! Clap! I turned around to face the bedroom door. Smooth came in clapping his hands.

"How long have you been standing there?" I looked at Smooth sideways.

"Long enough to hear you lie to your husband." Smooth sat down on the edge of the bed.

I hopped out of the bed with the sheet still wrapped around her body. Smooth wasn't going to get any more of my goodies. He tried to grab the sheet off my body. I popped his hands and moved away from him.

"First off that will be the last time that I lie to my husband. Smooth last night can't happen again. And another promise me that you won't tell anyone. I am a married woman." I grabbed me something to wear, lying it out on the bed.

"Look you know that I don't won't my mouth. What do you mean that it's never going to happen again? Ciara you know that you enjoyed yourself last night. I can tell by the way that you was throwing your ass back."

"Smooth you still cocky I see. Don't get it twisted, you caught me off guard when I was vulnerable. If Kanye finds out about this it would fuck up everything. I have to get ready, Kelly will be here soon."

"Kelly isn't coming, I told her not to worry I got this."

"Smooth why did you do that? You know that I a lot of running around to do. Who is going to help me with the children? Plus I don't have a car." Ciara whined.

"My mom can keep the children, besides Kelly has to work and run her business. Don't worry about a car, you know that it's plenty of those. You can drive my G Class that I have put up. I'm not taking no for an answer. Get dress, we're waiting on you downstairs baby." Smooth smacked me on my ass as he walked out of the bedroom.

Right now was not the time to argue or go against Smooth demands. Besides it would best if Smooth's mother watched the children instead. She didn't have anything else to do but sit in the house. I jumped in the shower lathering up my towel. Last night was on my mind, the soap filled towel paid more attention to my vagina more than any of my other body parts. Being considerate of everyone's time, I didn't take long. I brushed my teeth, threw my hair in a ponytail and dressed in a Nike legging set and sneakers. When I walked down stairs my children ran to me and gave me a big hug. Smooth cleaned off the kitchen table, he fed them making sure that their bellies were filled. I know at times that Smooth and I may have had our crazy situation's, but he was damn good father when he wanted to be. We all left out the doors, Eric Jr. was excited to hear that he was going over his granny's house. I was more than surprised to see that Kenya was happy. Whatever Smooth did it worked because at first she wouldn't even utter a word to or around him. Smooth made it to his mom house, it was very lovely on the outside. He purchased her this home three years ago. When I walked inside Ms. Jackson gave me a big hug, making me very emotional.

"Ciara it's very nice to see, it's been such a very long time. I'm so sorry for you loss Dear." I choked up and started crying again. "It's going to be just fine, your mother is in a better place now." Ms. Jackson rubbed my back, giving me a piece of tissue to clean my face.

"Thank you for keeping an eye out on the children. This is my daughter Kenya, she's allergic to peanuts."

As I was talking to Smooth's mother, Erica and Variyah came down the stairs. "Ciara! Ciara! I miss you so much!" Erica ran up to me giving me a huge hug.

"Oh my God, is this you Erica?! You've gotten so big on me. I miss you so much too." Hello pretty." I said to Variyah, Kayla's daughter. She looked just like her mom, but still favored Smooth.

Erica gave her brother a hug and told all the children to follow her. Eric Jr was the only boy, I made sure that I told them that he isn't allowed to play with dolls or makeup. Ms. Jackson assured me that she wouldn't allow any of that behavior to happen under her roof or supervision. Although Eric Jr knew better, it had to be said. Smooth asked his mom for his car keys to his Benz truck. She gave Smooth the keys and we walked outside to his mom three car garage. The garage door opened, inside was a Lexus, Cadillac truck and the Benz truck. Smooth pulled it out of the garage, stepped out and given me the car keys.

"I'm following you. It's already filled up with gas. Where are you stopping off at first?" He asked me.

"My first stop will be the church so that I could set up the funeral arrangements. After that I'm going by the funeral home, and florist. Smooth you don't have to go with me, I can call Kelly."

"You can call her if you really want her to be with you instead, but I'm still not leaving you alone to do this."

"Fine you can still tag along, but I already text Kelly and told her to meet me at my mother church."

I jumped inside the truck and drove to the city. The traffic was light so it didn't take time for me to make it to the city. When I pulled up to the church, Kelly was parked in the parking lot. Smooth pulled in a parking space next to the both of us. We all walked into the church, I had to meet with the pastor and first lady of the church. They both were very polite and gave their condolences. By my mother being a dedicated member of the church, her funeral service was free and the choir will sing her favorite song. We set a day and time for Saturday morning, a week from now. I thanked them for everything, I can see and feel the sincere love that they had for my mother. The next stop was a place that I didn't want to face. It was hard for me to step inside the funeral home. We all sat inside the funeral director office going over arrangements. Corbin's were preparing my mother's body, she had to be embalmed. I signed the paperwork so that they had permission to pick my mother's body up from the morgue. That was a quick thirty minutes being inside of there. I was starting to get hungry and so was Kelly.

"Smooth, Kelly and I are going to get a bite to eat. I want to thank you for everything that you have done so far, but I'm fine from here."

"Cool with me. I will give you a call this evening beautiful. Here is my black card, lunch on me."

Smooth handed me his black card while he gave me a kiss on the forehead and hug. We were standing on a very busy Madison street as the cars drove by. He walked me to his truck, making sure that I was good. I was starving and craving seafood, when I lived here Smooth and I would always go to Devon Seafood + Steak. That's where I will be having lunch today on Smooth. As Kelly and I pulled off, my phone started ringing. For a moment I forgot that I was married, it was my faithful husband calling me. I chopped it up very quickly because Kanye knows that I don't care to talk on the phone while I'm driving. At this time I tuned everyone out, only focusing on eating. When I became hungry I could turn into a bitch. Driving in silence on my way to Oak Brook I just cried. Never, have I thought that I would be returning back to Chicago to bury my mother. My mother was young, only 54 years old. She let a disease get the best of her. If only she would've said no to alcohol. If only should would've moved to Arizona so that I could keep an eye on her. If only we would've been closer like a mother and daughter were supposed to be. Funny how your life can change in a matter of seconds.

As I was driving down Madison, I couldn't believe my fucking eyes. You have to be kidding me, this bitch was in town. It was too much traffic for me to whip a u turn in the middle of the street. By the time that I was able to turn right on Central Ave. and come back up Washington she had pulled off. So Smooth want to play these old mother fucking games with me again. I always knew that he wasn't truly over Ciara, but I didn't think that he would play second to her husband. I hit Smooth up immediately. Instead of getting irate over the phone, I asked him where he was at. Oh no baby he was not going to take me back to the old Kayla. Out here acting a fool over his ass, like I used to do. I made it to his bar in less than twenty minutes. Stepping out of my white Porsche truck in my Jimmy Choo sandals, I strutted inside my baby daddy bar. Security spoke to me, I smiled and waved as I kept it moving to the back of Smooth's office. He was on the phone talking conducting business. I sat down politely, crossing my legs and arms. I was steaming on the inside and was ready to explode. Smooth didn't make it any better once I found out the caller on the end of the phone was Ciara.

"Alright baby, you know that my mother doesn't have a problem with keeping her grandson. Ciara buy whatever you need for the children. Okay I'll talk to you later." Smooth ended his phone call with that heifer Ciara.

Rolling my eyes, "So you're really going to disrespect me like that? What the fuck is she doing her? When were you going to tell me about your girlfriend being in town?"

"Kayla I think that you're delusional, because I don't have to tell you a mother fucking thing. But, since you asked, Ciara's mother died."

"What does the death of her mother have to do with you? How did you two hook up, last time I know, you two were beefing with one another. What are you two back together again, is Ciara still with her husband? If she is, that means that you're her boyfriend." I laughed but I was fucking serious about their situation.

"It's none of your business what Ciara and I have going on. That's your problem, you're always worried about everyone else business but yours. That's why your business isn't successful right now."

"Here we go again, you taking up for that bitch Ciara. When she say jump, you're taking flight. Smooth she hasn't been here taking care of you. She doesn't suck your dick like I do."

I strolled over to Smooth, unzipping his pants. He didn't stop me as I placed his dick inside my warm mouth. Smooth grabbed my freshly styled weave shoving his dick deeper into my mouth. His phone rang continually, but that didn't stop us. My head game was strong, my motive was to suck the money out of him. Moments later it didn't take long for Smooth to shoot his white, thick nut down my throat. After he was finished, he patted me on the head.

"Good job, I needed that." Smooth stood and zipped up his pants.

My dumb ass was still on my knees like I was one of his fucking pets. Smooth talked and laughed on the phone to whomever the caller was. Getting up from off the floor, I tried to eavesdrop on his call. From what I heard fucked me all up inside. The conversation was all about her, Ciara this, Ciara that. I stormed out of his office with tears in my eyes. Leaving out the back door instead of the front to avoid his security. After all these years I meant nothing to Smooth, absolutely nothing. How could he do this to me? Why the fuck is Ciara here fucking up everything? I made it to my car sitting and plotting on my next move. I had to get my hands dirty, if I wanted Ciara to disappear from out of Smooth's life forever. Taking Smooth's advice, I took my ass up to my shoe store, Head Over Heels. It was time for me to put in some work and get down to business. Smooth wasn't going to give me the money, but I was planning on getting it by any means necessary.

Chapter Four

"Honey I'm home." I kicked off my gym shoes and threw down my bag. My home was quiet, Ant or my children wasn't in sight. I walked around my home searching for my family whom I miss very much. I was so damn tired, running around with Ciara was very exhausting. Finally I heard my family down in the basement. Apparently they were playing some sort of game because they were laughing and talking loudly.

"Hello, hello family. What are we doing down here?" I walked down the basement steps to find Ant and the kids playing a game on Wii.

"Mommy come play with us." My daughter Jasmine came running toward me pulling on my arm.

I was tired as hell, but I couldn't tell my family no. We played a few rounds before Ant put the children to bed. We both soaked in our hot tub together, while sipping champagne. Ant was very quiet as I rambled on and on about the day that I had with Ciara. That was not like my husband at all. I looked into his eyes noticing a look that I knew so well.

"What's going on Ant? You know how long that we've been together, I can see that something is wrong."

Ant stepped out of the hot tub, extending his hand to me as I stepped out as well. He wiped me down with the oversized bath towel, wrapping it around my body. We walked into our bedroom having a seat on the bed.

"Ant what's up, please don't keep anything from me. Did something bad happened today? Keep it real with me right now babe."

"Bae some shit went down with one of my connects in the street. He got bumped and he's in federal custody right now. Shit no looking good right now." Ant plopped down on the bed.

"Okay, relax. Do you have enough product to push? I'm willing to help you out anyway that I can. You know that our bank accounts are both full now, so money isn't a problem."

"Kelly it's not about that. It's about him being in custody, I just pray that they Mexican doesn't talk. You know how some mother fuckers get in a jam and start running their mouth. Fuck! Fuck! Fuck!" Ant shouted.

"Look calm down, before you scare the twins. I'm sure that we will just fine. Right now let me take care of you, help put a smile on your face."

I raped Ant taking his dick like I haven't had sex in a year. I was frustrated, he was upset. We both needed to make love to take it all away. Little did I know how big of problem that we had on her hands.

Today was the day of Ciara's mother funeral, Brenda was truly loved and missed. Ciara didn't take it very well. Her husband Kanye was here by her side. Smooth was there as while, low-key mad but he hid it well. I don't know why he felt that he had another chance with Ciara just because he spoiled her with cash and gifts. That's nothing major when you're dealing with a boss woman like my best friend. The funeral and burial was over, the repast was at the church hall. Everyone was there to support Ciara, Denise, Tia was in town, London, Ciara's assistant and friend, even Aaliyah was there. Over the years Aaliyah grew cool with us. She changed into a good person, plus Ant and Vell made us get along. All of our children were together at one time under the same roof. It's sad that it had to take a death for everyone to reconnect.

"Excuse Kanye, do you mind if I steal Ciara for a minute?" I asked, I could see that my best friend needed me.

"No I don't mind at all Kelly." Kanye kissed Ciara softly on the cheek.

We walked off, going into one of the rooms in the back. Tia, Denise, London and Aaliyah were already waiting inside. When we stepped in we all gave Ciara a huge group hug.

"Thank you everyone for being by my side." Ciara cried into our arms.

"Anything for you sis. We have forty five minutes left until it's over. Do you want us to spend more time with you back at your mother place?" I asked her.

"Yes, that will be nice. Too much is going on right now and I would love to catch up with you all." Ciara smiled, her eyes were puffy and red.

Everyone agreed, by five pm it was a wrapped. Everyone cleared out and to be honest I was so happy that it was over with. When we made it to Ciara's mother house we all got comfortable. Eric Jr. was with Smooth and Kanye and Kenya went by his family house. Ciara was fine with it all, just wanting to be with her friends at the moment. We all white wine, chilling and laughing at the old days. It was funny when we Aaliyah and I laughed about the moment when we were about to fight at Denise barbecue.

"Girl, I was one second from fucking you up. You better thank Ciara for stopping me." I laughed tossing a throw pillow at Aaliyah.

"Yes Kelly was ready to stomp you Aaliyah. I begged her to calm down and not to do it at Denise house." Ciara laughed.

"Lawd, I was so afraid that you two were going to mess up my apartment." Denise laughed.

All of us were having a good time. Everyone caught up with one another lives, sharing all their children precious moments. It felt cool to be among my girlfriends and catch up. My cell phone rang, it was Ant calling me. I excused myself from the living room, taking my call in private stepping in the kitchen.

"What's up bae?" I smiled, happy to hear from Ant.

"Baby I'm minutes away from the house, I think the feds are following me." Ant sounded overwhelmed.

"Are you serious Ant? I'm on my way now whatever you do, please don't go to the house."

I hurried back inside with the ladies. "Ciara can I please talk to you in private for a minute."

Ciara got up, joining me in the kitchen. "What's up Kelly? Is everything fine, why do you look like something is going on?"

"Ant just hit me up saying that the he believes the feds are following him. I'm so sorry sis but I have to go. Please don't be upset with me, I hope that you understand." I paced the kitchen back and forth nervously.

"Kelly that's not good, not good at all. You have to go and take care of your business. What's going on Kelly? You know what never mind, feel me in later." Ciara gave me a big hug. "Get out of here, call me when you can. Thank you for everything sis."

"You're welcome sis, I'm so confused right now." I grabbed my purse, said goodbye to everyone leaving out the door. I called Ant as I hit the highway, "Ant where are you? I'm flying down the expressway right now."

"I'm just riding in circles right now, they're still following behind me. Their fucking with me Kelly, that mother fucker Mexican ran his fucking mouth."

"Look just don't go to the house, meet me at a public spot. Where are Jasmine and Justin?"

"They're in the backseat knocked out in their car seats. Meet me at Walmart by the crib, in the parking lot."

"Ant, I'm twelve minutes away."

I drove seventy miles per hour trying to make it to my family. Right now was not a good time to be involved in some bullshit. Everything is going so fucking good right now. My real estate company, Global Real Estate was taking off. Last year alone I made ninety thousand, this year I was planning to make more. When I pulled into the Walmart parking lot, parking next to Ant. He was on the phone talking to Smooth before hanging up he told him that he will meet him shortly.

I looked around trying to see if I noticed a suspicious vehicle. "Are they still around, did they stop following you?" I asked him taking my children out of the backseat.

"They stop following me on my way to here, they're in a black Impala. Kelly I'm going to meet up with Smooth. Leave the twins in the backseat and let's switch trucks."

"No problem, where are you going?"

"I'm going to meet Smooth at the spot. I don't have any idea how long that I will be out. Call me when you and the children make it home. I love you so much baby, everything is going to be okay." Ant gave me and the twins a kiss. I didn't want to let Ant go, but I know that he had to take care of business. I jumped behind the wheel trying to lose my strength. This was a part of the game that I fucking hated. This was only the beginning of a bad nightmare. When I pulled on my block, I saw the black Impala parked a few houses down in the cut. Keeping a straight face, I drove into my driveway and pulled into my garage. The Impala drove past me slowly. I looked straight ahead, cutting my eye at them. The look on their faces was a surprise, they were looking for Ant. I pulled into my garage, taking my children out and into the house. After sitting them on the couch I called Ant.

"Babe, they were sitting a few houses down waiting on you. No they didn't fuck with me, when they realized that it wasn't you, they screwed up their faces and drove off."

"That means that they are looking for me. Kelly I know that you don't want to hear this right now, but I'm going to be out of sight for some weeks. Business only, besides I can't let them take me in front of my children."

"I understand Ant, you have to do what's best for your family."

"As of now a lot of things are going to change. You already know what time it is, we talked and prepared for a situation like this. Right now I need you more than ever. I will be contacting you soon when I get to my destination. Kiss my daughter and son for me, I love you all so much. You my Queen Kelly, don't you ever forget that."

"I love you too Ant, be safe King. I'll hold everything down for you."

I blew Ant a kiss before ending the call. The twins were lying on the couch still asleep. I held them both in my arms crying hysterically. How could all of this be happening right now? For all the years that I've been involved with Ant, we have never been apart. Times like this will show you how much a person is really down for you. I love Ant with all my heart, he's my husband and nobody is going to take him away from me. Not the judge or streets, I will go to war for my family, they're all I got.

I walked into Global Real Estate with my brief case in my hand. My assistant, Courtney was sitting at her desk. "Hey Courtney, are they still here?"

"Yes they are sitting in your office." Courtney said with a scared look on her face.

Before I stepped inside my office I prepared myself for whatever these mother fuckers wanted. "Good morning, how are you two gentlemen doing today?" I plastered a fake smile upon my face.

"Good morning Mrs. Fuller, I'm Agent Davis. I'm doing just fine now that you have graced us with your presence." Agent Davis gave me a sinister smile.

"How can I help you Agent Davis?" I took a seat, crossing my legs.

"I have some questions regarding your husband, Anthony Fuller."

"Why are you asking me about my husband, why not ask him instead?" I smiled.

"I'm asking you because he seems to be out of sight and not easy to find. Please if you don't mind, have your husband to contact me. I may have a great deal to offer him." Agent Davis gave me his business card.

I took the card out of his hand as my work phone rang. "I will do, now if you don't mind Agent Davis I have some homes to sell."

"I see that you have such a prosperous Real Estate Company. I would hate to see you lose it all over your husband. Have a great day, Mrs. Fuller."

Agent Davis left my business, having me feeling antsy. That last comment was a threat and I'll be damn if they bitch ass take everything that I work hard for. I took my phone call from a potential buyer and set up a showing for the weekend. Throughout the day I couldn't concentrate on my business. It has been a week since I've heard from Ant. By lunch I decided to close an hour early for the day. Courtney was concerned to see the Agent here and wondered why I was giving her the day off early.

"What is going on Kelly? Why was an FBI agent here this morning? Do I have to be concerned about my job, is everything okay?" Courtney asked me with fear in her eyes.

"Courtney you have nothing to worry about it. Your position here at Global Real Estate is secure." I told her.

"Look, I heard about Agent Davis from the hood. He has a high record for putting people away for a very long time. I'm not naïve, you do know that I'm from the same area as you. I may be younger and educated, but I'm still from the streets. I hope that you and your husband have a very good lawyer Kelly." Courtney gave it to me straight.

"I knew that I hired you for a reason, you're a mini me. Courtney you've been working here since the very beginning. We've grown to be like sisters, although you're taller than me. I'm still the big sister." I laughed, but continued. "Yes, my husband and I did get ourselves into a jam, but trust me I got this. Agent Davis or the FBI don't scare me. They will have to try very hard to take my family down." I told Courtney.

"I hear you Kelly, let me know if you need my help with anything. I know people that know people." Courtney laughed.

"Child get your young tail out of here. Let's go, enjoy the rest of your day." We walked out of my real estate office laughing.

I set the alarm and locked the doors. Global Real Estate was inside of an office suite building near the United Center. As we walked out of the building I looked around before I got inside my truck. Courtney pulled off first and I took off behind her. I had no idea that I was being watched. The only person who I could call and trust was Ciara. Thank goodness my best friend was up. I mean it was a fucked reason why she was up here, but everything happens for a reason. Instead of calling her, I popped up at her mom place. When I spoke with her earlier she mentioned that she wasn't going anywhere today. Making sure that I wasn't being followed, I circled around the area for a few times. Ciara was dressed down, wearing a scarf on her head, a tank top and some leggings.

"Girl I'm so happy that you are here. I'm going through my mother things. I could use some extra hands." Ciara said stepping to the side to let me in.

"Where is Kanye and the kids?" I asked Ciara before taking a seat.

"Kanye had to go back home, you know he's working on a major project. Kenya is upstairs sleeping and Eric Junior is still with his grandma. What's up, why are you acting like something is wrong with you?" Ciara said.

"Great we are alone, Ciara it's so much bullshit going on right now. One of Ant connects got popped and in custody. He snitched and now the feds are fucking with us. Last week they followed Ant but he shook them. Today one of the agents came by my company asking for him." I said.

"No way are you serious, why are you just now telling me this Kelly?" Ciara took a seat next to me.

"It gets worse, he made a slick comment about me losing my company because of my husband. Sis, I haven't heard from Ant in a week. The last time I did he was with Smooth." I said.

"Ok let me contact Smooth, I spoke to him earlier but he never mentioned any of this." Ciara pulled her phone out to call Smooth. She spoke in code, nodding her head to whatever he was telling her. She ended the call with him and looked at me.

"Good news, Ant is safe and cool. First we have to get you a flip phone before you can contact him. From now on you are not to talk about anything illegal on your IPhone. Second I'm going to make a call to Kanye. His cousin is an FBI agent, maybe she can help us out. Third we have to take care of your assets. What I need you to do is take all of your money out of the bank and close the accounts. I will open up a new one for you in my name." Ciara said.

"Thank you Sis, let me get my banker on the phone right now." I said.

"Wait, not on that phone. Here use my flip phone." Ciara gave me her phone. I called my banker, he closed my accounts but I wasn't able to get my money until two days. After that we went to Walmart and I bought myself a flip phone. Ciara called Smooth to tell him what was going on. We met up with Kanye's cousin that was an FBI agent, Leslie at Starbucks. She was cool and very helpful with my situation. She put her job on the line by telling us confidential information. Emilo Estevez gave up Ant name and many others in exchange for a deal. She said that they don't have anything on Ant, that's why they're following him so he needs to watch how he moves. Everything was all making sense and I had to get in touch with Ant soon. Ciara and I met up with Smooth at his bar, from there he told me where Ant was. He was two hours away in Champaign. I managed to speak to Ant on my new cell phone. He wanted me and the children to spend the weekend with him. Throughout the week I handled all the personal affairs. Ciara opened up a new checking account for me to hold my money. I left about fifth teen thousand in my account and the same in Ant's. The feds wasn't going to come and take away my bread, my home or my real estate company. I wasn't going back to the hood for no mother fucking body.

Thursday night after putting the twins to bed I just laid down in silence. I did something that I haven't did in such a very long time. There were many times in my life when shit was crazy. I always went to GG and she would pray. I still had her raggedy bible that she had for many years. Getting down on my knees I cried and prayed for protection over my family. After I prayed my cell phone rang, the caller put a smile on my face.

"Hello, hey brother. I miss you so much." I said wimping on the phone.

"Lil Sis, what's up? What the fuck happen in Chicago? Do I need to come there?" My brother said.

"Shawn it's so much bullshit going on right now. I have to call you back from my other phone, so answer." After breaking everything down to Shawn he booked a flight from Cali to Chicago.

Chapter Five

With all the craziness that was going in Chicago, it was a fresh of breath air to get away from Chicago. Leaving Eric Jr, back at home with his grandmother, Kenya and I took a flight back home. Although I still had some business to take care of back in Chicago, I decided to surprise my husband. Since Kanye had such a busy work schedule and couldn't stay long in Chicago, he would be happy to see us. The Uber Black car pulled up in front of my beautiful luxury home. We lived in Scottsdale, AZ, in a huge 4,985 square foot home. As soon as we stepped inside Kenya jetted off to her bedroom, she couldn't wait to play with her toys. I kicked off my shoes and walked around my home. As I walked toward the back I could hear jazz music playing softly. The closer I walked to the back, I could hear voices, laughter and music. It was a fact that Kanye was indeed at home. Not only was he at home, Kanye had a visitor with him enjoying our outdoor pool. The looks on their faces were priceless when they both saw me.

"Surprised to see your wife?" I cocked my head to the side. The Chicago Westside girl was about to come out of me.

"Ciara honey, I can explain." Kanye stuttered as he pushed away the brunette white woman.

She turned around, I recognized her face. Kanye and Chelsea, Scottsdale Tramp were both naked in my pool. I pulled out my phone and took pictures of this bullshit! I needed plenty of evidence for my lawyer because I was divorcing Kanye ass. Chelsea face turned beet red as she stepped out of the pool. I grabbed the towels and their clothes tossing them in the pool as I continued to take pictures.

"Please stop taking pictures. I'm truly sorry, I'll pay you whatever. My husband can't find out about this!" Chelsea begged me.

"You tramp, white, raggedy bitch is fucking everyone but your husband!" Punch! I punched that bitch in the face. She ran off crying holding her bloody nose. I walked off behind her to go get my Beretta out of the closet shelf. Kanye was behind me wrapped in a towel. I took my gun off the safety, pointing it at him.

"I loved you! I gave you my heart and this is how you betray me? By fucking a white whore Kanye? Six years, six mother fucking years, I've been nothing but the best wife and woman by your side. While your wife was back at home burying her mom, you rushed back to fuck your whore! In my house that you built for me and your family!" I cocked my gun.

"Ciara please don't shoot me, I'm sorry baby. It only happened once, it will never happen again. Just put the gun down baby so that we can talk." Kanye begged.

"One time is all it takes!" I cried. Suddenly I heard Kenya come down the stairs. "Mommy! Mommy! Do you want to have a tea party with me and my dolls?" Kenya said. She was carrying her dolls in her arms.

Kanye looked at me with pleading eyes as sweat dripped down the side of his head. "Don't do this in front of our daughter." He whispered. Kenya was one step away, I lowered my gun and tucked it under my shirt.

"Daddy! I didn't know that you were here." Kenya ran to her father, jumping into his arms. "Daddy I miss you so much. Do you and mommy want to have a tea party with me?" Kanye carried her off into the living room. "Daddy just came from a swim princess. Why don't you let daddy get dressed first and I promise to join you." Kanye said.

Kenya kissed him on the cheek and ran off back upstairs. I shook my head, he was blessed that Kenya was here. If not his brains would be all over my gorgeous marble floors. Kanye walked over touching my shoulder.

"Don't you put your fucking dirty hands on me bastard! As a matter of fact, get your shit and the fuck out!"

"Baby, please don't put me out. I promise that it will never happen again." Kanye dropped to his knees begging me. He grabbed my hand and tried to kiss it.

Smack! "You damn right it won't happen again because I'm leaving you. I will not allow another man to ever hurt me again. You of all people know everything that I've been through with Eric and you go around and do the same exact fucking thing! I hate you! I want you out of my home and out of my life!" I walked off with Kanye chasing behind me.

Every word that he was fucking say was irrelevant at this moment. I don't know where the hoe Chelsea ran off to and don't give a fuck. I'll deal with that bitch later for fucking my husband. Kanye and I were in our bedroom, I helped him moved faster throwing his clothes out of the closet.

"I'm not going anywhere Ciara, not until we talk about this." He said.

"Talk?! Let's talk about how disrespectful you are by fucking a bitch in our home. Not only did you disrespect me, but you disrespected my children! You are a fucking embarrassment! Between the both of you, money isn't a problem. You could've at least booked a room to fuck your whore! Kanye you don't care about me or our marriage. I don't want to hear shit that you have to say! Just get your clothes and leave, you can come back for the rest of your things at another time."

Kanye got dressed and took a few things with him. I didn't even bother to ask him to leave his keys because I was changing the locks. After he left I broke down crying. That shit fucked me up inside seeing him with another women in our pool. Damn, after everything that he and I had built, it was going to be hard to walk away from it. Right now I was very confused and didn't know what to do. I sent the pictures of him and his mistress to my email to save them. Kenya called for me and her father from her bedroom. Snapping out of it, I washed my face so that she didn't see me like this. I'll be damn if I go through this with my daughter, my little girl will never see this side of life. I walked into the room with Kenya who was sitting at her table along with her dolls.

"Kenya sweetie I was thinking that you and I could go have lunch at Chuck E Cheese. Is that alright with you?" I asked her.

"Yes momma! Let's go, I love Chuck E Cheese!" Kenya yelled in excitement.

"Alright let's go, but promise not to tell your brother. This is a mommy and daughter date okay."

"Okay momma I promise not tell my big brother."

I gave Kenya a kiss and a hug, never wanting to let her go. We walked out of the house to Kanye sitting inside his car. He refused to leave I see. Kenya who was crazy about her father ran off to him. I followed behind her, she invited her father to Chuck E Cheese with us. Kanye agreed to go as if he was invited by me.

I interjected, "Don't you have some business that you need to take care of?"

"Plans changed, I'm free for the afternoon." Kanye smiled slyly.

I just exploded on his ass, "I will not continue to play these childish games with you Kanye. Now please go on by your business! I don't want to see your stupid face right now!" I was trying my best to not curse in front of Kenya."

We both continued to go back in forth of Kenya that she stopped us. "Mommy, daddy can you please stop fighting." Kenya said covering up her ears. Taking a look at our daughter, we kilt the arguing.

"This was exactly what I was trying to avoid. That's why I asked you to go away." I said to Kanye. I bent down to kiss Kenya on the forehead, "I'm sorry sweetie, mommy and daddy will never argue in front of you again." We walked away toward my car. I looked back at Kanye, "You can go with us, but in separate cars.

When we made it to Chuck E Cheese, Kenya and Kanye went to play games. Time from time Kanye would try to talk to me, acting as if everything was cool. I couldn't wait for this play date to be over with. Kenya started yearning, it was time for us to head home. On the way out Kanye asked me if we can talk. He didn't talk no for an answer, I was so upset to see him parked in front of the house. The only reason why I didn't beat him back to the house was because I was on the phone talking to Kelly. I didn't get a chance to tell her what all went down because she was talking about Ant's situation. I carried Kenya into the house to lie her down. Now was the time for round two. Kanye was sitting down on the couch prepared to talk. I took a seat across from him, looking him straight in the eyes.

"It's taking everything in me not to kill you right now. What you did was the most disrespectful thing ever. It's like déjà vu all over again with Eric. How long has it been going on? How many women has it been?" I wanted and needed to know answers for me.

"You're right, it was such an awful thing for me to do. I've only been seeing her for a three months. It started when I her husband and I begin to work on the project together. I'm truly sorry, I wish that I've never did it to begin with." Kanye said.

"Three months ago." I slightly chuckled. "You're willing to risk everything that you worked hard for by fucking your partner wife? What if I didn't come home and caught you in the act? The affair between the both of you would still continue. The trust is over between us, I don't think that I could ever trust you again." I said.

"I don't want to break up our family Ciara. Please give me another chance, look I don't even have to sleep in the same bed as you. If you want me to I'll just sleep in another bedroom." Kanye begged and pleaded with me.

I paused and thought about the great sex that I had with Smooth in Chicago. At this moment I no longer regretted bouncing up and down on Smooth's dick. Kanye caught a ghetto blessing this time.

"You have to give me my space and stay out of my way as long as we're both living together. Besides I have to spend a few more weeks in Chicago anyway."

"Are you selling your mother's house?" Kanye asked.

"No I'm not, that will be my home in Chicago whenever I visit. I just need to tidy up somethings around the house. I'm leaving this weekend, the plan was to surprise my husband and not walk into a surprise." I rolled my eyes, got up and walked away.

I went into our bedroom, locking the door behind me so that Kanye wouldn't join me. Mentally I was drained from it all. From my mother's death and my husband's betrayal. Stepping inside my marble shower, I allowed the water to beat down on me. I cried as I thought about my mother abusing me when I was younger. All I could think about was her telling me that I was black and ugly. Catching Kanye with a white woman made me feel insecure about my complexion. When I stepped out of the shower I could hear Kanye jiggling the door knob. Ignoring him. I applied baby oil to my body. My smooth dark chocolate skin was beautiful. I received a Facetime call from Smooth. The loyal Ciara who loved her faithful husband wouldn't have answered his call. Not that things have changed, I answered his call as I stood there naked.

"Hey baby daddy." I laughed as I stared in his face. Smooth eyes went from my face down to breast.

"Damn baby, you making my dick hard. When are you coming back to Chicago?" Smooth asked my breast.

I snapped my fingers to get his attention. "My face is up here, I'm coming back this weekend. How is Eric Jr. doing?"

"He's good, just hanging out with his family. I'm taking him and the girls skating this weekend. I wanted to know will Kenya be back."

"If that's the case I could book a flight for Friday. Besides. I miss my son and you very much." I said.

Smooth took it all in staring into my eyes before he responded to my comment. If anyone knew me, he certainly did. "What's wrong Ciara? Just the other day you were against me and you getting back together. Now you miss me, what's going on?" Smooth face turned serious.

"Nothing is wrong, it's just that spending time back in Chicago brought back memories. Memories of the good times, when I first met you." I lied to Smooth

Smooth brushed it off, continuing to talk about our son. I promised him that I would be back on Friday instead. I tried to tease him with my sexy body, but Smooth wasn't having it because I didn't want to discuss my issue with him. Getting upset I ended the facetime call in a polite way. There was no need to be upset with Smooth about me and Kanye infidelity problems. Ten minutes later I fell asleep alone in the bedroom that I once shared with my husband. Kanye continued to twist the door knob trying to enter.

Chapter Six

Watching my wife leave to go back to Chicago with my daughter was the hardest thing for me to witness right now. Over the last four days I begged and pleaded with Ciara, but she wasn't trying to hear shit that I had to say. It was hard to be under one roof and to be separated from your wife. Everyday Ciara teased me walking around the house with less as possible on while Kenya was at my parent's home. At night I would sit on the other side of the locked bedroom door as Ciara slept alone. Today was now the day that she was leaving me again to be with her first love. Right now going back home while things were fucked up between the two of us was not a good idea. The thought of Ciara and Eric getting back together was heavy on my mind. Ciara strolled out of the house with Kenya by her side.

"I'll call you as soon as I land Kanye."

"When will you be returning home Ciara?"

"I'm not sure about that, but it will be before the children start school. Besides, I think that right now we could both use you space. You need to think about the bullshit that you pulled honey." Ciara batted her long eyelashes.

Kenya gave me a hug and a kiss before she hopped into the car. She was a child and didn't have the slightest clue that her mother and father were fighting. As Ciara and I went back and forth with one another, she interrupted us. "Mommy can we please go now, I miss my big brother and really want to see him." Kenya whined.

At the moment the bickering stopped between me and Ciara. I closed the car door and watched Ciara drive off to her life in Chicago. Kenya looked out the back window waving goodbye to me. At the moment I realized that I fucked up everything by being unfaithful. Ciara is the type of woman that could hold a grudge for a very long time.

When I arrived to Chicago this time Smooth was waiting for me at Ohare. Kelly was busy dealing with her situation with Ant. Smooth was sitting in his truck with all of his children. His son and daughters Erica and Variyah. They all were happy to see me and Kenya. Kenya was very excited to see her big brother, giving him a hug and kiss. Smooth opened up the car door for me, being the gentlemen that he was. Riding next to him in the Chicago streets made me feel like we were a couple again. The whole day Smooth took the children off my hands allowing me some free time. I went to get my hair done by my old stylist and bumped into a few old faces. One of those faces wasn't too happy to see me. Kaylah stood a distance from me as I spoke to an old friend in the beauty shop after the stylist finished my hair. She had a mean mug upon her face, if I was her I'll be mad to if I was her. Kaylah looked tired and unhappy, word around town was that her little shoe boutique wasn't doing well. After I was done talking to an old friend, I prepared to leave. When I walked past Kaylah she rolled her eyes as she sat down in her seat like the punk bitch that she was. Before I made it to Smooth's Benz truck, Kaylah came walking out of the shop.

"No matter what you just can't stay away. You always have to come running back trying to fuck things up with your messy ass." She walked up behind me saying.

I turned around to face this miserable bitch. "Kaylah don't worry about me, worry about your fucked up life that's hanging by a thread. Five years later and you're still just a miserable lonely bitch. You want to be me so bad, but it'll never happen. I suggested that you find someone else time to waste. I got money to make, something that you don't know anything about." I walked off stepping into the Benz truck.

That only hurt Kaylah feelings causing her to show her jealously and rage. Before I could pull out the park she starting yelling and screaming at the top of her lungs. She jumped on top of the car pounding the front window. Guess who face time called my phone while all the craziness was going on? That's right Smooth aka as our baby daddy. As soon as I answered he could hear all of the foolishness that was happening.

"Ciara what's all that noise that I hear? Is everything cool?" Smooth asked.

I changed the camera on his stupid ass baby mother, Kaylah who was on top of the car. "Do you see what I have to deal with? Just because she want to play with me, I'm going to give her a game." I pulled off driving with her on the hood of the car. Kaylah kicked her freely legs, holding on to the windshield wipers trying not to fall.

"Bitch I'm going to fuck you up!" Kaylah yelled.

I laughed and turned on the windshield wipers which caused Kaylah to hit the ground. Everyone watched and laughed at her silly ass. I rolled down the window, "You're a goofy bitch! You better be thankful that I'm not spiteful enough to run you over." I shook my head and sped off down Western Ave. leaving that dumb bitch in the dust. Smooth was still on the phone trying to figure out what was going on. I explained everything to him, but I wasn't concerned about Kaylah and neither was he. My only concern was the children that was the only reason why I spared Kaylah's life. I knew that her daughter loved her mother, she was only a child that was caught up in all this mess. Smooth didn't want to discuss the situation in front of the children. We both agreed to discuss it later on, right now I had to check on my business. I met up with London at my boutique in Oak Park to go over my new business plan. I parked the truck and checked it for damages. It was only a few dents and scratches that could buffed out. My hair and I was still fabulous as I strolled into my Bella Boutique Illinois location.

"Hello London!" I walked over to give my friend and business partner a hug.

"How are you Ciara? You look great, you rocking that wrap girl." London said.

"Thank you darling, I'm doing fine. Just taking it one day at a time." I looked around the store and noticed the changes and a new fresh face. She smiled at me as she stood next to the All-White Section of clothing. London introduced us, "Ciara this is Alicia, I just hired her part time to help out in the store."

"Hello Alicia, I'm Ciara the owner of Bella Boutique. How are you doing?" I asked her politely shaking her hand. Alicia was young, dark and very pretty. She wore her hair in a bob that made her high cheekbones pop. She smiled showing off her pearly white teeth.

"OMG, it's such a pleasure to finally meet you. I've heard so many good things about you from my boyfriend Bobby, he works for Smooth." Alicia smiled and said.

"Yes, I know Lil Bobby and that was nice of him." Two customers came into the store so I couldn't continue my conversation with Alicia. "Alicia we can talk another time, Welcome to Bella Boutique and it was a pleasure to meet you." I smiled and said.

"A pleasure to meet you as well Ciara." Alicia walked off smiling as she assisted the two customers.

London and I stepped into the office to discuss business.

"I feel like that Bella is missing out on something London. You know me very well and I've been thinking that we should add lingerie and swimwear to our collection."

"That's a great idea and I've been thinking the same. It will be great to do because they're isn't too many black owned boutiques selling swimwear and lingerie." London said.

"I have the suppliers already, what I need you do is help me pick out the pieces. I only want to carry maybe ten pieces of each. I want them in all of my stores." I said.

"Great, how soon do you want to make this happen?" London asked.

"ASAP, here are the items. All we have to do is choose which one to put in Bella's." I gave London the IPad and told her to check out the items. She smiled and loved most of the things that the supplier was offering.

"These are some very nice pieces, hell I'll even rock me a few items." London laughed as she gave me a high five.

"Girl I knew that you would like my idea. We need to make a decision by the end of the week, place an order and have the items by next week." I said.

"Cool and do you want to do promotional marketing for the swimwear and lingerie?" London asked.

"Yes, we can set up a photoshoot. I need three models, slim, thick and plus size."

"Great, I can make that happen." London wrote down everything as I talked. "As a matter of fact Alicia could be one of the models, the slim one."

"You're right, she would look nice." London asked Alicia to step in the back for a second. Alicia came to back to join us. I asked her if she would like to be Bella's Boutique featured model. She happily said yes and started to cry. I didn't know the young girl that well, but a part of me felt close to her. Alicia seemed sincere, soft and sweet, but I could tell that she was dealing with something on the inside. I will get to the bottom of that later on, but right not I was happy to be a positive change in her life.

Two hours later, after my meeting with London I decided that I covered everything. I treated both her and Alicia to lunch. Alicia even helped out picking some very nice pieces. She also shared with me that she was going to school for Fashion Design.

"It was fun hanging out with the both of you. Alicia welcome to Bella's and a part of the team. London I will give you call tomorrow dear." I gave both of them a hug before leaving.

During the two hours while I was there Smooth called to check on me. I let him know that I was cool and didn't allow that Kayla incident to upset me. When I made it to my mom house, I was able to relax and chill alone for a few hours. I thought about Jasmine and my mother as I sat alone inside the house. Even though it has been years since Jas death, she will stay come to me when I was stressed out. Kelly was the only person that I shared that with. Jas would come to Kelly all the time as while. Tonight I wasn't alone like I thought I was when Jas appeared. She sat across from me at my mother's dining room table as if she was alive. I wasn't afraid, in fact I was really happy to see her.

"Hey Sis, how do you feel?" Jas asked me.

"Jas, I'm so happy to see you. You know that I have so much going on right now. My mother's death, Kanye's infidelity and," Jas cut me off.

"You having feelings for Smooth again?" Jas laughed as she mentioned that.

"How do you know that I'm feeling Smooth again? Sis, you aren't even here, oh my God if a dead person can see it, so can anyone else." I joked.

"Ciara you know that I know you and Kelly like the back of my hand. Although I'm not in the land of the living, I'm still pretty much alive in your lives. If this will help, Smooth still loves you, he never stopped loving you. But, Kanye loves you as well and he is sorry. As a matter of fact he will be calling you tonight so be prepared and take time to hear him out." Jas said.

"Can you love two people at the same time? Is that even impossible or normal? On one hand I love my husband and on the next I love my son's father. I'm so confused Jas, I don't know what to do." I said.

"I trust that you will make the right decision. Enough about the men, how do you feel about the death of Brenda?" Jas touched my hand.

My eyes began to water up, Jas rubbed my hand. "Let it out Ciara," she said.

"I hate the fact that I wasn't there for her. She was my mother and I should've been there for her. I blame myself for leaving her behind. I wish that I could've been more involved in her life, that she spent more time being a grandmother and that she didn't have to go back to alcohol." I cried as Jas held my hand.

"Ciara you can't blame yourself for your mom's death. Please don't beat yourself up for that. Brenda is in a better place now, being here was very hard for her. She may be dead, but she will forever be with you." Jas hugged me.

"Jas thank you. I love and miss you so much. I wish that you were still here. Girl I ran into crazy Kaylah today and it went down."

"Sis no. Please don't tell me that she's still acting crazy over Smooth." Jas laughed and said.

I continued to talk to Jas like she was still alive. I had to fill her in on all the crazy moments that I had in life. Jas and I laughed so hard, just like the good ole days. She drifted off when Kanye called me, but before she left she told me that she loved me, giving me a big hug. I answered Kanye's call and just like Jas said he had a lot to talk about. Being a good wife, I listened to everything that he had to say. He wanted to work on our marriage and start all over. I told him that he had to do marriage counseling when I return back home. If I was going to continue our marriage we had to talk to someone, get help. Maybe I should consider counseling for the death of my mom too. Smooth returned to my motherhouse with Eric Jr. and Kenya, who both were sleep. He helped put them to bed and made himself comfortable.

"Well crazy Kaylah is still up to her drama I see." I just jumped right into it even though I didn't want to but, it had to be addressed.

"Kaylah and I have nothing going on. We had a talk earlier about the situation and she regretted making a fool of herself out in public."

"She damn sure made a fool of herself. Anyway forget her, Smooth we have to talk. I want to thank you for being here for me during my mother death. You have been such a big help, with the children and making sure that I get around. I'm confused what exactly are we doing?" I asked him.

"Ciara you know that I want you back more than ever. I know that you're not happily married. At first you we're, but now I don't see that love spark that you had for Kanye. What I see is that we're falling back in love with each other. You can't had it baby, what are we going to do?"

Smooth kissed me and I didn't stop him. He was right, I was falling back in love with him. I wanted my Chicago life back. It was last stressful than being with my unfaithful husband in Arizona. My children seemed happier here and it felt good being close to Kelly and a few other old friends. Smooth had me feeling loved again. Kissing the side of my neck, caused my nipples to harden and my pussy to get moist. He knew every hot spot on my body, just the right places to get things popping. I unbuttoned my blouse and removed my bra. One by one he kissed and sucked on both of my succulent breast. We were both caught in the moment until I heard a very soft familiar voice from the top of the stairs.

"Mommy, Mommy I can't sleep, Mommy why is my brother father kissing on you?" Kenya rubbed her sleepy eyes as she stood at the top of stairs watching her mother with another man.

"Oh shit!" I mumbled under my breath. Quickly I grabbed my shirt putting it on, as I ran toward Kenya. "It is okay baby, let me help you get some sleep." We walked back into the bedroom. How was I going to explain to my four year old daughter what she just witness. Kenya was too sleepy to ask me a several questions. As I rocked her back to sleep she held on to me tightly. Awful thoughts of me being such a terrible mother went through my head. I laid her down and found my way to my mother's bar that she had in her bedroom. Brenda was doing some serious drinking to have a bar right next to your bed. I poured myself a shot of Hennessy, one shot wasn't enough. I took down another shot. Finally the bad thoughts went away. After that I heard a noise behind me, I turned around to see Smooth standing there.

I paused to look at him, "You're still here? I thought that you left." I softly spoke.

"No, I'm never leaving you baby." Smooth said as he stared at me with lust in his eyes.

I walked past him to close and lock the bedroom door. This time I couldn't risk my children walking in on me having sex again. Door locked, clothes off, pussy wet like Aquafina, and dick harder than wood. Smooth and I fucked all night long.

Chapter Seven

It was hard to keep the tears from falling. Ciara stood by my side as I watched Ant get handcuffed and read his rights. The Feds showed up to my house and with a search warrant fucking up my place. Ant tried to get away but the caught him one block away from the house. I was thankful that our son and daughter was in childcare to not witness this bullshit. Ciara restrained me keeping me calm so that I didn't get arrested. You know that I acted a damn fool on them son of a bitches. Those white pigs laughed taking pleasure in destroying my things. One of the agents come from one of the bedrooms upstairs carrying two bricks of cocaine.

"Look at what we have here?" The agent held up the bricks. He walked over toward me prepared to handcuff me.

"That isn't mine! Your crooked ass planted that!" I yelled.

He wasn't trying to hear shit that I was trying to say. He read me my rights and threw them handcuffs on me. "Keep it cool, I'll call your lawyer and make arrangements." Ciara said.

I spoke in code as they walked me out of my house. Ciara understood what I was saying and got on top of her business. She had to leave and grab my children from childcare. I sat in the back seat of the car calmly as they took me to the station. They took me in a room where two agents tried to question me about the drugs and Ant. After they realized that I wasn't going to talk, in walks Agent Davis. I never said a word to him as he threw nasty insults and threats at me. One hour later my lawyer showed up.

"Kelly, please don't say a word. I see that you're busy trying to arrest innocent people." My lawyer said to the federal agents.

"Innocent, once again you client is guilty. We were just trying to cut her a deal so that she doesn't have to spend time in jail." Agent Davis said.

"My client has every right to sew you and your crooked department. We have evidence of your agents planting the drugs in my client home. I suggest that you get ready to go to trial." My lawyer and I walked out of the building.

Ciara had come through, I had cameras all over my home running 24/7. I can have access to my home activity through my email and on the app on the security company. When I was being hauled to jail, I told Ciara what to do and to get in touch with my lawyer. I knew for a fact that I didn't have drugs in my home. Ant and I never would have drugs around our twins.

"Kelly I have good news and bad news. The good news is that we are going to sue the hell out of them and will win. The bad news is, I wasn't able to get Ant out as of yet. Unfortunately, they are still questioning him." My lawyer said.

"Please do whatever it is that you have to do Blass to get Ant out." I said.

"There is a witness that's willing to testify against Ant. As of now they're looking for something solid on him. I will try my best to have him out soon, as of now I suggest that you go home. I will call you once this all settled." Blass said.

I called Ciara to come and grab me, but she couldn't leave my home unattended. She sent Aaliyah to pick me up instead. "Thank you Aaliyah for coming to get me. I'm surprised that you and Red are still in Chicago." I said.

"I'll be leaving in two weeks. I have a very busy interior decorating business to run. Red wants to stay for a few more weeks. I'm burnt out with Chicago, just letting the twins enjoy time with me and Red family. Red told me what was going on, it's a duffle bag in the trunk he told me to give you." Aaliyah said.

"Cool." I used the GPS on my phone for navigation, so that Aaliyah knew how to make it to my house. During the ride home I was a nervous wreck. My mind was racing and I was very concerned about Ant. When I arrived back to my place, to my surprised I had a visitor who I wasn't expected to see until this weekend. It was my brother Shawn. I ran and cried into his arms.

"It's alright Sis, this is small to a giant." Shawn kissed me on the forehead. "I'm here now and will handle everything."

We all went in the house, Me, Aaliyah and Shawn. Ciara was sitting upstairs with my children in their bedrooms. They're rooms wasn't that bad due to the raid. I rushed to give them a hug, assuring that everything will be just fine. We all sat in the living room talking about what my next plan was. First I had to get my home back together, next I needed to worry about Ant. Apart of felt like he was good, but I knew that I was going to be out of a lot of money for his freedom.

I had to call a meeting with Red and Vell regarding Ant. They had him in federal custody and he didn't have court till next week. When times like this occurred we looked for family, because we all were family. Under no circumstances Kelly was going to go through this alone. Our major problem was the witness and getting rid of him. Word was that he was in protective federal custody, but for a price he could still be touched. With the help of my cousin who worked for the FBI, we were aware of Emilo Estevez location. My next step was getting the hit arranged under the radar. This wasn't a difficult task, but it was time consuming. The hit had to be successfully done and can't be traced back to us. Emilo was incarcerated in a highly secured facility in Colorado. That's when Shawn, Kelly's brother came step in. He was a cool dude that had a lot of dealings with the Mexicans in his time.

"Smooth everything is set up, the cost is twenty thousand." Shawn puffed on his cigar, the smoke circles danced in the air.

"He'll get half right now and the other half after it's done." I said.

"That can be arranged." Shawn got on the phone to make the call. He spoke in Spanish. I see that Shawn has grown a bit in a lot of ways. He placed the caller on speaker phone, we didn't know his name. He had deep Spanish accent, this time he spoke in English.

"Wire the money to my girl Jenny. Once I get half, give me twenty four hours. After the hit you have less than an hour to wire my girl the rest of the money." The hitter said.

"Done!"

Monday morning I received a phone call from my cousin at three am. Rubbing my eyes, I answered the phone call.

"I'm wearing all black." My cousin said, that was code that hit was successful.

"Good copy." I said hanging up the phone.

I sat up in bed, disturbing my beautiful lady as she slept on my chest. "Is everything good?" Ciara asked me.

"Yes, everything is great. I didn't mean to wake you black bone. Let me handle this business real quick."

Stepping into my living room I made the call so that the other half of the money could be wired. He was on it, I hit Red and Vell telling them what went down. Ant next court date was next week. I was expecting to hear from him today when he called me from his cell phone that I had supplied for him.

When Smooth walked out the room, I quickly pulled out my phone to call Kelly. She answered in her sleepy voice. "Sis wake up, it's me Ciara." I whispered into the phone.

"Ciara what time is it?" Kelly asked pausing, "Its 3:11 am, are you and the kids cool?" Kelly panicked.

"The kids and I are fine." I whispered. "It's done Sis."

"Yes! Yes! Yes!" A happy Kelly yelled into my ear.

"Shhhhhh, calm down Sis. I'm sneaking on the phone to call you while Smooth is in the other room. We'll talk in the morning, now go back to sleep. Love you." I whispered laughing.

"I love you too Sis, talk to you later." Kelly ended the call.

Smooth was still in the living room on the phone. The sound of a vibrating phone caught my attention. It was coming from under the pillow that Smooth was sleeping on. Lifting the pillow up, it was Smooth's other phone going off. Now, I haven't gone through a man's phone in years. Honestly I trusted Kanye enough to never go through his phone. You see how that turned out to be for me. The devil on my left shoulder was telling me to go through his phone. As it continued to vibrate, I picked it up. It was several messages from psycho Kaylah. I read all five of them, she was confessing her love to him. Her text messages were so dreadful to read. Kaylah begged Smooth to be with her and she hated on me as well. You know I was a few bitches in the texts. After not getting a response back from Kayla took it upon herself to text Smooth pussy shots.

"Oh hell nawl." I almost threw up. It took so much in me not to reply back to this thirsty trick. Smooth was coming toward the door, I placed his phone back under the pillow. Rolling over pretending as if I was asleep. Smooth got back in the bed, he felt his phone vibrating under his pillow. I peeped out of one eye to see what he was going to do. Smooth grabbed his phone, looked at the texts and erased them. I smiled, it felt good to know that he didn't have any feelings for Kayla. You know that I haven't been around for five years and anything could've occurred between the two of them. Smooth laid down, my slick ass rubbed up against him. He kissed me on my forehead, cuddled with me and we both fell back asleep.

When my flip phone rang, I nearly broke my neck to answer it. The only person that called me on that phone the most was Ant. I was so happy to hear from him. "Hey husband." I answered when I opened the phone.

"Hello wife, how's my family doing? I miss you and the children so damn much." Ant said.

"We're doing fine, Jasmine and Justin are eating breakfast in the kitchen with Shawn. How are you doing is the question?"

"I'm doing fine, just waiting for Bliss to come by and see me. He said that he some great news for me." Ant threw that out there, but we both already knew what that great news was.

"Great news sounds good to my ears right about now." I said.

"Did you get the house cleaned up? Can you put the children on the phone? I would like to talk to them."

"Yes the house is clean, I paid a company to come and clean up the mess. We lost a few things, but nothing that couldn't be replaced. Give me one second, let me call the children to come in here." I called Jasmine and Justin upstairs to come speak to their father on the phone.

They were happy to hear from their father and asked him when will he be home? Ant told them that he didn't know. He spoke to Justin on the phone a little longer than Jasmine. After they were done talking on the phone. Ant and I talked on the phone for another five minutes.

"Sweetheart I promise when I get out of this jam you and I are taking a trip." Ant said.

"It would be nice to get away, you, me and the children." I said.

"I was thinking just you and I Kelly. We can take the children to Walt Disney World or something. It's been a very long time since you and I have did something together. Don't get me wrong I love our children but I also miss the days before we had children. We can have some adult fun, just me and my beautiful wife. I want to make love to you on the beach in Bora Bora. You deserve that and more, my queen."

I started to cry. "I love you so much. I was trying not to cry and be strong about this whole situation. These last two weeks without you have been crazy. I don't know what I will do without you. I'm just ready for all of this to be over with." I cried.

"Baby don't cry, it will be over soon. I love you. I'll hit you later on tonight queen." Ant said.

"I love you too king…kiss kiss." I ended the call.

Ant absence made me appreciate it him even more. I must admit at times we both go so hard for our children that we haven't thought about ourselves. I was so busy with my Real Estate Company and he was so busy with his multiple business. I cried as I thought about the times we shared. The precious moments of me having our children. Ant was there for everything, never missing a beat. Tomorrow Jasmine had her hip hop dance performance. Ant wasn't going to be there, but I was going to record it for him.

Justin ran into my bedroom excitedly, "Momma I beat Uncle Shawn in 2K16." When he saw that his mom was crying he came over to me. "Don't cry momma, I'm the man of the house until my daddy gets back. What do you want me to do to stop you from crying?"

Justin made me chuckle. "Come here big boy and give your mom a hug." Justin was tall and slim like his father. He was taller and mature than the average five year old. He gave me hug as he rubbed my back. "Do you feel better now momma?"

"Yes I do, much better. Now I'm the tickle monster." I laughed and begin to tickle Justin. His laughs were so loud that Jasmine came in to join us. I tickled both of them until they double teamed me and began to tickle me. Shawn stood by the bedroom door laughing at us. I sent the kids off to attack him. Shawn fell to the floor as his niece and nephew tickled him. Family was everything to me, through the tears, laughs and cheers.

Chapter Eight

My family and I were in the middle of enjoying our Sunday dinner when an unexpected visitor popped up. 'Ding Dong, Ding Dong.'

"Are you expected anyone Kelly?" Shawn asked me.

"No I'm not, maybe it's Smooth." I said

Shawn got up to see who was at the door. She didn't waste any time barging through the door.

"How is everything Kelly? As soon as I heard what happened with my son, I hopped on the next flight." Marilyn said.

Surprise, surprise Ant mother is back. Let me feel you in on Marilyn really quick. Over the last five years we have saw Marilyn here and there. She would always pop up unexpectedly in our lives. It was no question that Ant was still in contact with his mom. I on the other hand, never reached out to contact her for any reason. It wasn't that I didn't like or care for her. What I don't care for is Marilyn absences in her grandchildren lives. Our children adored Grandma Marilyn and was happy to see her.

"Grandma! Grandma!" Jasmine and Justin ran over screaming to their grandma.

"My precious little lambs, grandma miss you so much." Marilyn kissed them both. "Hello Shawn, how are you?" she asked my brother.

"I'm doing fine Marilyn, how about yourself?" Shawn asked.

"You know me. I've just been chilling." Marilyn said.

I rolled my eyes, Marilyn never wanted to act her age. She was in her fifties and still popping. From the looks of things she's had some surgery done. Nothing with her face, she always looked pretty young for her age. Her breast were sitting up, waist was small and her butt stuck out. Shawn was checking her out. I slapped him on his arm, snapping him out of his trance.

"Kelly are you okay daughter? Ant called and told me everything. He told me that I didn't have to come, but I refused to not come and see about you and my grand babies." Marilyn gave me a big hug.

I hugged her back. "It was all crazy at first, but I won't be fine until Ant comes home."

We all took a seat at the dining room table as I filled her in on everything that went down. Marilyn ate and soaked up the whole story. After that she asked me if it was fine if she stayed here with us until everything died down. I didn't mind at all, besides I needed the help with the children since Ant wasn't around to help. Marilyn and the children were happy to hear that she was staying with us. I didn't take long for her to start her grandmother duties.

"Come on grand babies, let me give you a bath. Then, after that you two can read me a bedtime story." Marilyn, Jasmine and Justin went upstairs to have some fun.

Shawn sat at the dining room table as I cleared it off. He watched Marilyn switch her ass up them damn stairs. "Brother you do know that she's old enough to be your mother right?" I laughed and said.

"I know, but that body is brand new." Shawn joked.

"That's just nasty, uughh." I played like I wanted to throw up.

"Speaking of mother's, when was the last time that you saw or talked to mom Kelly?" Shawn turned serious.

"It's been a while, but I've been so busy with everything that's been going on. It's not as if she isn't on my mind. I make sure to send her money and pictures of the children every month Shawn."

"Do you know that she's up for an appeal soon Kelly?"

"Another appeal, isn't this her third one?" I said.

"Yes it is, this time I got her a better lawyer and she has a great chance on getting out. She's been doing really good things in prison. She also has been on good behavior for the past five years. She may be coming home this year. You need to reach out to her Kelly, soon." Shawn said.

Quietly I continued to place the dirty dishes into the dishwasher as I thought about what Shawn had just told me. I do recall my mother saying that she was coming up for another appeal this year. Every time she spoke of it I would just dismiss the thought of her coming home. She's been out of my life for so long, that I've been slowly moving on without her. Shawn could see the regret in my eyes.

"She's waiting on you to reach out to her Kelly. I'm going to get myself a room at Hotel Arista. You should be fine now that Marilyn is here to help you out with the children." Shawn gave me a hug and went to gather his things.

Once he was done, I watched him leave as he loaded his luggage into the trunk of the rental car. "I'll call you Shawn, love you brother." Shawn said, 'Cool little sis, and love you too." Before getting in the car and driving off.

When I returned back inside Marilyn was inside my fridge looking for something to eat. She was wearing a gray onesie and a black hair bonnet on her head. I shook my head as I watched her search inside my fridge. Marilyn pulled out some fruit preparing to make herself a fruit salad. I pulled up a chair at the table, popping a grape into my mouth.

"So Miss Marilyn what have you been up to for the last year that's kept you away from your son and grand children?" I jumped right into the questions.

Marilyn huffed and puffed, rolling her eyes and shaking her head. "Well Miss Kelly, just jump right into it I see. Well I've been getting my life together. You know working on my mind, body and soul in Minnesota. I know that's not really an excuse to be missing in action, but in my defense I have been talking to Ant. Kelly I'm sorry that you and I are not close, but from here on out I will like for us to creating a bond. Do you think that you and I could do that?'

"Sure Marilyn, I have no problem with you at all. I just don't like your disappearing acts that you pull. If you promise to be around more we can grow a bond. It's not all about me, my children love you so much and need you. I'm happy that you're are here for us, but can you try to be a better grandmother for Jasmine and Justin."

"This time I'm in it for the long haul. I know that I wasn't the best mother to Ant, but I promise that I will be the best glam ma from now on." Marilyn said.

"Glam ma? Marilyn you're something us." I laughed.

"Yes, I still got it girl. I had to get my body right Kelly." Marilyn took a spin for me so that I could see her new body. All I could was laugh at her.

"Marilyn does Ant know about your new body?" I asked her.

She looked at me with her sneaky look. "No he doesn't know yet. You missy will not tell him either. Hopefully he won't be upset once he sees me."

"I don't think that he would care. He'll be so happy to see you instead. By the way you look great, I might have to get myself some nip and tuck." I laughed.

"Kelly your body is fine. Your skin is glowing and you look so youthful." Marilyn complimented me.

"Thank you Marilyn. Well I'm off to bed, I have houses to sell tomorrow. Goodnight."

"Goodnight daughter." Marilyn said.

As I walked upstairs Marilyn made herself comfortable on my sofa to watch television. How could Ant not share with me that he had spoken to his mom? In the back of my mind I always felt as if he was always in touch with her. If she thought being under my roof was going to be a vacation she had another thing coming. I always let Marilyn off easy in the past when it came to being a grandmother. Not this time around, I was going to put her ass to work. I showered, after that right on cue my flip phone started ringing. It was Ant calling, I answered quickly.

"Hey bae." I smiled.

"What's up beautiful? I'm surprised that you're still up. Long day with the children?" Ant asked.

"I was a long day filled with pop ups. Your mother is here. Why didn't you tell me that she was coming Ant?" I asked him.

"I thought maybe you needed the help until I got home. I didn't mean to stir up things. Kelly you better be nice." Ant said.

"Oh it's no problem with me, your mom is always welcomed here. Enough about her, Ant I miss your big dick so much." I moaned into the phone as I rubbed my clit.

"Damn babe, you making daddy dick rise."

In the morning I woke up bright and early. Marilyn on the other hand was still sleeping. I made breakfast for everyone. The aroma of the food awaken Marilyn. She walked into the kitchen rubbing her still sleepy eyes.

"Good morning grandma." A cherry Jasmine and Justin yelled.

"Good morning babies." A groggy Marilyn replied.

We all sat at the table eating breakfast. Every time when Jasmine and Justin played amongst one another I took notices that it irritated Marilyn.

"Children that's enough back and forth. Go upstairs and get dressed for child care." I said.

Jasmine and Justin ran off upstairs to get dressed. I laughed at the two of them as their tiny legs took off.

"Marilyn you must a well wake up and get yourself prepared for your grandchildren. I'm getting ready to leave out now. Here is the address of their day care. A list of what they're allergic to. Plus my number to my job, Ciara and Shawn number as well if you need to contact them for help and can't reach me. Also I need you to pick up some more food for the house" I handed Marilyn a sheet of paper.

"Please don't tell me that you're putting me to work already. I just got here, I thought maybe that I would have the first day to myself. Please Kelly don't do this to me." Marilyn said.

"Oh no honey, you see last night when I talked with Ant. We both discussed that you were here to help me out until he gets back. Am I wrong or am I right?" I looked at her sideways.

"You're right. Okay let me put on my granny role and get my act together." Marilyn snatched the paper out of my hand.

"Thank you, that's more like it. Oh by the way I need your cell number and email address." I said.

Marilyn looked at as if I was crazy. "Email address?"

"Yes so I can email you the list that I just gave you. I'm not trying to hear that you didn't know about anything when it comes to Jasmine and Justin."

Marilyn looked afraid and like she wasn't up to it. I knew that Marilyn and children didn't really work. The reason why it never did was because she always ran from a commitment. She was going to face reality right now or she's not welcomed in my home. I called Jasmine and Justin downstairs to give them instructions before I left.

"Yes momma." They both said at the same time.

"I'm leaving for work now and leaving you in the hands of your grandma Marilyn. I expect you two to be under your best behavior. If I hear that you gave her a problem, there will be consequences. Do you understand me?" I told them.

"Yes momma." They said.

"Alright, now give me a hug. I love you so much. Momma has to go make some money now."

As I left to go to work, I noticed that Agent Davis was in the cut. He followed me from a distance as he tried to blend in with traffic. I called Bliss to inform him that Davis was fucking with me.

"Bliss, Agent Davis is following me. I'm more than sure that he's going to visit me again at my company. Can you be there just in case he decides to visit me?" I asked.

"Sure, I'll meet you there." Click.

Agent Davis followed me all the way to work. When I arrived Courtney and my lawyer Bliss was already there. I told her what was up so that she could be prepared. We resumed during our duties at work until Agent Davis arrived. He was surprised to see my lawyer present with me when I stepped out of my office to greet him.

"Why do keep on harassing my client?" Bliss asked him.

"Oh, I was just stopping by to let her know that her husband got off lucky this time." Agent Davis said.

"What are you saying? Anthony is being released?" I acted as if I was surprised.

"I don't know how he did it. I'm keeping my eyes on you." Agent Davis threaten me.

"You have no right to threaten my client. As a matter of fact you're not allowed to be around her because of the lawsuit that she has against your department. I suggest that you find someone else to harass if you want to keep your job." Bliss told him.

Agent Davis chuckled as he left out of my company. I stuck my middle finger up at him as he walked out the door. After that Bliss and I discussed my legal options. Everything started off fucked up and suing the system was my next step. The Federal department was willing to settle with me for only twenty five thousand. I declined that offer and was going to trial, they had to be fucking kidding me. The time that I would've gotten for the planted drugs was ten to fifteen years. They were going to pay for what they crooked ass tried to pull on me.

Throughout the day I called to see how and what Marilyn was doing. She was busy grocery shopping and running errands that I requested. I made sure that she didn't forget to pick up the children, so that I could just head straight home. When I got off work it was a car accident on the expressway, which led me to get home forty minutes late. When I arrived home I was tired but blessed and happy to what I walked into. Marilyn cooked dinner, lasagna, with broccoli and garlic bread. They all were sitting at the table like one happy family. I was pleased that Marilyn took it upon herself to cook. Before joining them I quickly showered, threw on some clothes and went to join them. Ant called us while we were in the middle of eating. He was more than happy to hear that everything was working out. Last night he begged me to give his mother a chance to be involved. I must admit Marilyn passed day one and if she keeps this up, I can see us getting closer. As Ant spoke to the children on the phone I thanked Marilyn for helping me today.

"Thank you Marilyn. You cooking dinner was such a big help today. I wasn't expecting you to cook." I said.

"No problem Kelly, that's what I'm here for. We're family and family is supposed to be there for one another."

What Marilyn said was true and had me thinking deeply about my mother.

Chapter Nine

Today was my annual checkup with my doctor of fifteen years. Dr. Willis was my primary physician and urologist. I always made sure that I took care of myself and went to the doctor on a regular basis. In the past I didn't have the best track record when it came to having safe sex. Now you couldn't pay me not to wear a condom. I don't trust these scandalous hoes period. Over the past five years I've had many women try to play the pregnant game on me. I knew that they were lying because I had a vasectomy. Now that I'm older, I don't play around with my life anymore. It's not about sleeping with a lot of women. When I was younger I fucked them all. Now that Ciara is back around, I want my family back.

"Hello Eric how are you today?" Dr. Willis walked inside giving me a hand shake. He was a great black doctor who had has own practice under North Western.

"I'm doing great Dr. Willis. Just great, here for my annual checkup." I said.

"How's your children doing Eric?"

"My children are doing fine. Ciara is back in town and so is Eric Jr." I smiled and said.

"Oh that's great. You have to bring them by. I would love to see the both of them it's been such a very long time. I can see that you're very happy yourself. Are they here to stay or is it just a visit?" Dr. Willis asked.

"Yes I am happy, unfortunately they are only here to visit for the summer. Ciara mother was ill and passed away."

"I'm sorry to hear that. How is she holding up?"

"She's taking it one day at a time. Dr. Willis before we get started I have something very important that I would like to discuss." I said.

"No problem, what's that Eric?"

"I want to have vasectomy reversal surgery." I said.

Dr. Willis took off his glass and sat down. "Eric are you sure that you want to do that? It is very possible, it's been four years when you've had a vasectomy. I will have to perform a test to make sure that you don't have a blockage and no antibodies in your sperm. Once the results come back, then we can go from there."

"I'm very sure and thought about it from sometime. Today we can perform whatever tests that you need to take. I would like it done soon, how long does it take to get the results?" I asked.

"The results usually come back in two days. Once it confirms that you are still fertile, I can perform surgery within that same week. Vasectomy reversal usually takes from two to four hours, followed by a few more hours for recovery from the anesthetic. It's an overnight procedure, you can expect to go home the next day. Pain is moderate and you can resume your normal activities, including sex, within two weeks." Dr. Willis explained.

"Wow, doesn't sound complicated at all." I said.

"Great, lets get started Eric." Dr. Willis said.

One hour later I was finished with my doctor appointment. While I was in the middle of my exam, my phone was ringing non stop with phone calls. We weren't allowed to use our phones in the doctor office, but Dr. Willis made an exception for me. It was my mother calling me, when I answered her voice boomed through my speaker.

"Smooth you need to get here as soon as possible. Ciara and Kayla are here arguing and about to fight in front of these children." My mother yelled.

"What? Are you serious? What is Kayla doing over there?" I asked my mom.

"She just popped over here without notice to get Variyah. If I would've known that she was coming by I would've had Variyah prepared to go home. Ciara and I were on our way out the door, taking the children to the Shedd Aquarium. When Kayla saw Ciara, she flipped out and tried to attack her." My mom said.

"Alright, I'm on my way there right now. I'm leaving the doctor's office right now." I ended the call. I was so upset and furious.

I left the doctor's office in a rage waiting to rip off Kayla's head. She out of all people know that I don't play about my mother. Out of the people for Kayla to disrespect my mother should've been the last person ever for her to cross. Kayla doesn't have anybody to help her. My mother has been there since the very beginning when Variyah was born. Ciara should be the last person that she's concerned about. As I rushed through traffic, my mother called me back.

"She left with Variyah. Eric I'm very worried about my granddaughter, she snatched her by the arm and tossed her in the car." My mother said.

"Don't worry, I'll just meet Kayla at her place." I said.

"Eric don't do anything crazy to jeopardize yourself."

"I won't mom can you put Ciara on the phone for a second?" I asked.

Ciara got on the phone. "Look I need for you to make sure that my mother is straight until I can get there. I have to take care of Kayla ass. After that I'll be by there." I explained to Ciara.

"Smooth be careful, Kayla seemed like she was high on something." Ciara warned me.

"Alright good looking out." Click.

I made a detour to Kayla's place, which wasn't too far from the city. She lived in LaGrange in a three bedroom home. Pulling up, I realized that Kayla wasn't there when I didn't see her car. Instead of waiting I parked a few houses down and waited for her inside. Luckily I had her house keys on me and didn't leave them at home with my other set. When I stepped inside Kayla's house it was clean. She purchased new furniture from the last time that I was over here. It looked as though she had help with an interior decorator, because the furniture was very modern and not Kayla's style. I took it upon myself to see if she had any food in the fridge. Just like I suspected her fridge was bare. The only thing that she had inside was containers of old takeout food a bottle of Remy. As I walked down the hallway, I passed Variyah's room first. My daughter had a full size Cherrywood canopy bedroom set that I purchased her. Her room was still clean with her princess comforter set and items. I loved my daughter so damn much, I just hated her mom. The next room was the guest room. Which had Kayla's old bedroom set inside of there and a flat screen on the wall. The next room was Kayla's, inside it was a mess. Clothes and shoes were everywhere. Old empty food containers and used condoms were on the floor. Empty wine bottles were on her dresser and so was a line of cocaine and ecstasy pills. Kayla had a new bedroom set as well. On her dresser I spotted one of Aaliyah's businesses cards. I knew that Kayla had help with decorating because the furniture was very nice and she didn't have any style. An older picture of the both of us and Variyah was inside a broken picture frame on her nightstand. No longer being able to stay inside her filthy drug infested room, I went back into the cleanest room in the house. I took a seat on the couch, waiting for her to arrive. Twenty minutes later the sounds of keys entering the lock caught my attention.

She walked inside with my daughter Variyah and Wendy's. "Daddy!" Variyah ran over and jumped into my arms.

Kayla wasn't happy that I was sitting inside her home. "Smooth what are you doing here? Look you need to get the fuck out now!" she walked up on me.

Placing Variyah down, I stood up in front of Kayla. I grabbed her by her neck, choking the air out of her. "Don't you ever disrespect my mother again, do you understand me?!" Kayla swung her arms for dear life. The cries of Variyah kept me from killing her. Throwing Kayla down like an old rag doll, she gasp for air as she rubbed her neck.

"I fucking hate you Smooth! Get out before I call the police on you!" Kayla screamed.

"Did you just threaten to call the police on me?!" Smack! Smack! Smack! I smacked the shit out of that silly bitch three times. Kayla cried harder, I picked my daughter up prepare to leave out the door.

Kayla grabbed on to my right ankle. "Where are you going with my daughter?" I continued to walk out of the door as I dragged Kayla with me. I shook her off my ankle, "Let me go coke head, you need to get your life together." I walked out of her house with Variyah in my arms.

As I walked down the street to my car, Kayla came rushing toward me with a butcher knife. By the time I saw the knife, she stabbed me in my right shoulder. "Bitch is you crazy!" this time I punched her like she was a nigga on the street. I hit her in the stomach, knocking the wind out of her. Kayla fell to the ground holding her stomach. I placed Variyah in the back seat and jumped behind the wheel pulling off. Blood ran out of my shoulder scaring Variyah, she was afraid that I was going to die.

"Please daddy don't die on me. You have a lot of blood on your shirt daddy." Variyah cried.

"Its fine baby girl, daddy will be fine. Just sit back with your seatbelt on. I'm taking you back to your grandma. Please don't cry, you're safe now."

I called Ciara instead of my mother, not wanting to worry her anymore. Ciara met me up at Adventist LaGrange Hospital without telling my mom. I was urgent care getting ten stitches while Variyah sat in the chair sucking on the lollipop that a nurse had given her. When she saw Ciara walk in she was excited to see her, jumping into her arms.

Ciara looked at with a worried look in her eyes. She didn't ask about the situation while Variyah was present. On the way home Variyah rode back with Ciara instead to my mother house. My mother was happy to have Variyah back at her place. Variyah was happy as well and so was Erica and Eric Jr. I prepared myself for my mother's preaching. It was the look in her eyes that gave it away.

"We have to have a serious talk about what happened today Eric." My mother said walking upstairs to her bedroom. Ciara and I followed behind her. "Eric, Kayla is never welcomed back over here. She performed like a fool up in here, not caring in front of the children. What's wrong with her, is she on some type of drugs or something? She almost knocked me down trying to fight Ciara. Ciara didn't want to fight her but, no she kept on trying to come after her. She doesn't have any respect for herself and nobody else. I'm not about putting the court in yawl business but, she isn't fit to care for Variyah."

"I agree mom, I will get in contact with my lawyer today about seeking custody of Variyah. What happened today will never happen again. Get you some rest, Ciara and I will take the kids with us for the rest of day. I love you." I kissed my mother on the forehead.

"You be careful out there with them children Eric. Tell Ciara to call me later on so we can talk. Love you too."

We left with the children and went back to Ciara's place. While we were there when Ciara received a phone call, she would press the ignore button. I knew that the caller was Kanye, what I didn't know was why she was ignoring his calls. Whatever was going on Ciara was going to tell me tonight. It was starting to get late and I wanted to get my daughters back to my mothers place. I also had to take care of some important business. So I just cut to the chase regarding Ciara and Kanye.

"Ciara why do you keep ignoring your husband's phone call? Is it because you're sitting in front of me?" I asked her.

"Smooth it's complicated and I really don't feel like talking about it right now." Ciara said.

"I can respect that, as long as he isn't hurting you. Well check out it, I'm going to take the girls back home. I'll hit you in the morning when I get up." I gave Ciara a kiss on the lips.

"Please tell me that you aren't going to be with Kayla tonight." Ciara said with a sad look upon her face.

"Kayla is the last person on my mind. Baby, I have a very important meeting tomorrow. I love you Ciara. You're all that matters." I said.

"You know I love you too, call me when you make it home."

We both kissed, I felt uncomfortable kissing her because she was married. By knowing her for so long I knew that she was having marriage problems. Ciara wasn't for lies or bullshit, I'm not going to lie. I'm happy that Kanye fucked up so now that I could have her back. Before Ciara and I can move on, she had to have her husband completely out of her system. I still love that woman and this time around I promise that I'm not fucking up again. First I have to handle this Kayla situation in order to have some peace in my life. The last thing I wanted is for Variyah to grow up fucked up like her mother did. I had to fight for custody of my daughter so that she didn't have to be around her coke head mother. I've given Kayla too many times and years to get her shit in order. She's not only stressing me out, now she's stressing out my mother. My mom loved her grandchildren very much. They all gave her life and a reason to keep busy. Not only that, my children were crazy about their grandmother. The second Eric Jr saw here again, he ran into my mom arms. He didn't want to leave, that was the only reason why he stayed with my mom and Ciara didn't have a problem with it. The only reason why Kayla pulled that incident with my mother was because of Ciara. It's never been a problem with Variyah ever being at my mother house. After today, she could forget about ever being alone with her daughter again, after I witnessed the things for very own eyes. Don't get me wrong I've heard rumors about her getting high but, I ignored them because she never gave me a reason to feel that she was getting high. After I dropped off my daughters, I sat back and chilled out the rest of the evening watching ESPN in my home alone.

Chapter Ten

"Damn where in the hell is Smooth at?" I asked Vell.

We were sitting at the conference table, waiting to start our meeting with our potential investors for our next business. Money wasn't really an issue but, in the south suburbs they weren't going to allow four African American men open up a profitable, successful business.

"I spoke with him this morning, he should be here soon." Vell said.

"I hope so, we already had to come up with an excuse for Ant not being present." I said.

Seconds later Smooth walked in. "Damn glad for you to join us." Smooth gave me a slight smile.

"Red and Vell I took an important phone call before stepping inside. I've been sitting in the car on the phone for the last five minutes. I saw you two calling but. I couldn't click over." Smooth said.

"Is he cool, I know that he has court in the am?" I asked.

"Yes he's straight, just wanted to run a few things by me first." Smooth said.

"Man where the fuck are these people at?" Vell said under his breathe, he wanted to be careful about speaking to loudly. You never know if they have you on camera.

Moments later the two perspective men walked inside. We all stood up and shook hands before discussing business. I presented them with a business plan with the opening of a sports bar in the south suburbs on the same level as Hooters. The only exception was that the focus on the women would be their asses and not their breast. The two Caucasian men loved the idea and was ready to invest in us. All we had to do was go over the contract with our lawyer before signing. They were giving us a week to get back in touch with them. We all walked out of the meeting shaking hands and happier men. This right here is life changing move for all of us. If everything goes right, we could break ground in a month and start building our restaurant and have the grand opening by the next summer. What we were doing was a money maker and a man paradise. Men from all over can come by and watch sports while being served drinks and wings by a beautiful woman with a big ass.

After the meeting, Smooth, Vell and I went to hang out at Smooth's place. When Smooth took off his suit jacket I noticed the bandage through his shirt.

"Damn what happened to your shoulder bro?" I asked him.

"Krazy Kaylah stabbed me yesterday. She went by mother house to get Variyah, once she saw Ciara she tried to fight her. It caused my mother blood pressure to raise." Smooth explained.

"You have to stay away from her before she fuck around and kill you. Doesn't crazy run in her family or some shit?" I joked and said.

"Yes and getting high does too. Kayla is doing coke, I saw it with my own eyes. You know that I can't have my daughter around that bullshit. All I could think about is, in the back of mind how long has this shit been going on. That important phone call that I was on this morning was me talking to my lawyer about gaining full custody of my daughter." Smooth said.

"That's fucked up, even though I stay out of all the women bullshit. I do hope that Kayla gets some help. Coke is serious habit to shake, you know I seen it kill both of my parents." I said.

We all took a moment of silence until Vell spoke. "Red how are the quads doing? I saw how big they've gotten. I know that they keep you and Denise busy." He said changing the subject.

"Raven and Rhianna are driving their mother crazy. Jayden and Jordan are keeping me busy. You know what though, I wouldn't trade my life in for nothing right now. They're fifth birthdays are coming up soon. Denise is renting out a space for their party. Now that all of our children are here, all of them can celebrate together." I said.

"Sounds like a plan, just have Denise get in touch with Ciara. It's about time to have all of children together." Smooth said.

For the next couple of hours we chilled out, watched sports and talked shit among one another. Ant called Smooth on the line talking shit on the speaker. He had court on Friday morning and was more than ready to get released. Everything was all fun and games until Smooth, hit Vell and I with a shocker.

"Aye, I went to the doctor yesterday. I'm in the process of getting my vasectomy reversed."

My drink blurted out of my mouth." Are you fucking serious? Please tell me that you want more children bro?" I said.

"Yeah, I want one more with Ciara guys. I plan on having one more with her."

"Does Ciara know about this, or are you just making this shit all up right now?" Vell joked.

"No serious guys, I haven't brought it to Ciara yet but, I'm sure that she wouldn't mind having one more with me. I know that I fucked up this time, I want my girl back."

"What's her husband name again....Kanye right? Whatever the hell his name is, he's going to fuck you up." I said.

"I don't think that Ciara is happy with her marriage. You know that we have been sleeping together since she has been back. We all know that Ciara don't carry on like that. Something is telling me that Ciara and Kanye would be divorcing soon." Smooth said.

"Bro, I'm on your side with you and Ciara being back together. I know how much you two are in love with one another. I just think that you too are too damn old to be having more children. You have two and she has one by you and another. Just do the Brady Bunch thing." I laughed, dabbing Vell.

"Having more children is some real shit to think about Smooth? Aaliyah and I are done in that department. She got her tubes tied, clipped and burnt. The twins will be graduating out of eighth grade next year, going to high school. I refuse to start all over again." Vell said.

Smooth went on trying to convince us into thinking that he was doing the smartest thing. All I'm saying is that, I'm not with the shit. To each its own though, he was my brother and whatever goes down I'll be there to support it. Honestly I always felt that Ciara and Smooth would be back together again. Smooth was playing with fire though, Kayla was still crazy about him and Ciara was still married. That whole entire situation was fucked.

"Be careful bro, when you're dealing with feelings everyone can't handle separation. Someone is liable to get hurt and I don't want that to happen to you." I said.

"Thanks but I got this bro. Trust me Ciara will be mine again so." Smooth said.

After working earlier picking and choosing which swimwear and lingerie that I was choosing, I decided to ask Kelly and Denise opinion. They both came by with their children to my mother house. I showed them the pieces that London and I picked out.

"Okay ladies, I need your honesty. Tell me what you think about these pieces.' I said.

I allowed them to take their time as they looked at each piece. I explained to them that I was looking for something classy and not trashy. Something that they wouldn't mind wearing at the beach or in the bedroom. They both had good taste in clothing, so their opinion really mattered to me. Kelly gave her opinion first liking eight out of ten pieces. Denise liked all of them, wanting to order a swimsuit right away. Right now I wasn't really thinking on how I could ask Kelly anything, her mind was only on Ant at the moment. I took both of their opinions into consideration but, I was keeping all the pieces that London and I choose, with the exception of one. I emailed London the choices and was ready to place the orders. We had a week to get the photoshoot and marketing done. Three weeks from now was my fashion show. I had a lot of work to do and no times for games.

"I have so much work to do ladies. I know that I initially come to Chicago to work but, since I'm here I decided to put together my idea. I've been thinking about this for a very long time." I explained to Kelly and Denise.

"I think it's a really good idea and different. Swimsuits and lingerie are a must now. Especially swimwear for all the people who travel to the warm places in the winter." Denise said.

"I agree with Denise. I see that you've got the place cleared out without a lot of your mother things. Are you planning on redecorating?" Kelly asked.

"Yes I am, redecorating and moving back." I said under my breath.

"What?!" Kelly and Denise both asked me at the same time as they looked at me like I was crazy.

"I'm leaving Kanye, he's been having an affair. I got him with his mistress at her home, in our pool." I said.

"Nooooo fucking way Ciara! I know that you snapped out right?" Kelly asked.

"Not like I wanted to because Kenya was there. If she wasn't there it could've been deadly. You know what though, honestly I don't love him anymore. I continue to pretend like I do, I've been feeling like this for a few months now. Kanye works all the time, barely spending time with his family." I said.

"Ciara how did the woman look and react when she saw you? Did she know that Kanye was even married?" Denise asked.

"Good question Denise. The other woman is his business partner wife. A white whore who's known for sleeping around a lot on her husband. To make the situation even crazier, every time when Kanye had to go out of town to work on a project. She was always there, but I was thinking that she was traveling with her husband. Not there to fuck my husband."

"Damn, I'm sorry that you have to go through this. Kanye was very disrespectful for fucking her in yawl pool. I'm not into fighting over a man but, she deserves to get her ass beat. I hate home wrecking whores!" Denise said.

"I'm okay, I just don't know how I'm going to break the news to the children. Right now their feelings are the ones who I'm concerned about the most. Moving back to Chicago will be a change for them. I can stay here at my mother place until I find another home."

"How's does Kanye feel about all of this. Has he been trying to get you back? Kelly asked.

"Kanye wants to work everything out by going to marriage counseling. He calls and emails me all day long. I don't want to talk to him right now. He even offered to buy me a new home. I don't care about him fucking her in our home. It's deeper than that, much deeper."

In the middle of talking to Kelly and Denise my mother doorbell rang. "Excuse me, maybe it's Smooth at the door. He said that he was on his way an hour ago." I got up to answer the door, to my surprise it wasn't Smooth. Before I could utter a word out of my mouth he kissed me.

Smack! "Kanye what are you doing here?" I said as I watched Smooth pull up in front of my mother house.

My heart started to beat fast, what the fuck am I going to do?" I thought to myself.

Chapter Eleven

"Excuse me, coming through. Ciara I'm going to run out to my car to grab something really quick." I said to Ciara as I slid passed her and Kayne.

"Hello Kelly, how are you?" Kanye asked me.

"I'm fine Kanye." I said dryly, rolling my eyes. I held my tongue from going off on his trifling ass. Right now I had to have my best friend back, Smooth was parked out front. I didn't need for shit to go down, not in front of the children. Playing it off, I walked over to have a seat inside the car with Smooth.

"Ok brother, let me explain before you start to thinking that you were set up or something." I said to Smooth.

"Sis, I know that Ciara wouldn't set me up to run into her husband. Just the other night she was ignoring that nigga phone calls." Smooth said.

"Smooth I just wish that you and Ciara would just get back together. Yes, Ciara and her husband are going through somethings. It's really bad that Ciara is getting a divorce. I know for a fact that you love her and that she loves you. You know that she's tells me everything. I know that you two are back sleeping together. That Kayla stabbed you the other day. That your mom wants you two back together. Look brother, Kanye fucked up so you better get up on it. I just hope that you're ready to be the man that's Ciara is in love with." I said.

"Why is Ciara and Kanye divorcing? If you don't mind me asking Kelly." Smooth asked.

"Now I can't tell you why, I'll let Ciara talk to you about all of that." My cell phone started ringing, it was Ciara calling me. "This is Ciara, let me see what's up." I answered my phone.

"What's up sis?" I asked Ciara.

"I'm in the bathroom, Omg is Smooth mad at me?" Ciara asked me.

"No he isn't, he's sitting right here. Would you like to speak to him?" I asked Ciara.

"Yes, put him on the phone." Ciara said.

Giving Smooth some privacy, I passed him my phone and stepped out of the car, so that Ciara could talk to him. Whatever they spoke about took ten long minutes. Smooth rolled down the window and handed me back my phone.

"Thanks Sis, I'm about to go now. I'll see you Friday on Ant's court day." Smooth looked sad.

"Are you alright Smooth?" I asked him.

"Kelly I'm straight. I'm going to allow Ciara to handle her business with dude. She'll get back at me once everything is settled down."

"Okay give me a hug." I hugged Smooth. "Don't worry brother, I got this." I told Smooth.

He laughed, "Your little ass crazy for real. Go back inside, I'll pull off when I see you step inside." Smooth said.

I went back inside, Denise was gathering her children preparing to leave. Ciara and Kanye were sitting across from one another looking crazy. Once again I stayed out of it and prepared to go home as while. Ciara was a grown women and knew how to take care of her business. Me and Denise said goodbye before leaving. On my way home Ant called me, I put him on speaker phone and talked to him. By the time I pulled up to my house, my children was sleep in the backseat.

"Bae I have to carry them inside the house, give me ten minutes and call me right back." I told Ant.

"Cool, answer your phone when I call back." Ant said.

"Don't I always answer silly?" I laughed.

I pulled up into the garage and ended the call. One by one I took Jasmine and Justin inside, lying them down on the couch. They little asses were heavy, damn near causing me to break my nail. Out of breath from carrying them, I took a seat on the couch. As I was sitting down in my quiet living room, I heard moans. The moans were coming from upstairs. I got up, the only person who could be fucking in my house is Marilyn.

"I know damn well this old lady bet not brought nobody in my house to fuck." I said under my breath.

Step by step, I marched up my carpeted staircase. The closer I got, the louder the moans became. To make things even worse, Marilyn didn't even bother to close the bedroom door. I walked inside my guest room to a shock of a lifetime.

"Omg! Marilyn! Shawn! What the fuck?!" I yelled. Covering my eyes, I ran out of the room and back down the stairs. "Lawd, why did I have to see it?" I said to myself.

Shawn came running out the bedroom and down the stairs. He was shirtless but, he had time to throw on a pair of jeans. "Kelly please let me explain."

"Ewwww! How can you explain my brother and my mother in law sleeping together?" I said.

Moments later Marilyn peeped over the staircase, afraid to come down the stairs. I shook my head as Shawn tried to explain. "You can come downstairs Marilyn, I'm not mad at you." I said. Marilyn came down the stairs fully dressed wearing the maxi dress that she had on earlier. Before she opened her mouth and Shawn continued to talk, I stopped them both.

"Look I don't agree with what I just saw but, you two are grown just like me. With that being said, I can't tell two grown people what to do. What I can tell you is to never let it happen again in my house, garage, backyard, hell anywhere on my property. I can't believe that you felt comfortable enough to even do this in my home. What if Jasmine or Justin would've saw you, then what? Please start thinking before you do things, because what you do affects everyone around you." I lectured their asses like I was their adult and they were the children.

My flip phone rung, it was Ant calling me back. I rolled my eyes and answered the phone, which was not a good idea because I was still riled up. "Hello!" I said into the phone.

"Damn bae, what's up? Why do you sound upset?" Ant asked.

"Do I sound upset, I'm not upset." I said, Marilyn grabbed my arm as she begged me not to tell Ant what just happened. I snatched my arm away from her and took a seat.

"I'm not upset. I'm cool, I just broke my nail while I was carrying the children in the house. It hurts like hell." I lied to Ant.

"Oh I thought something else was going on. Like I was saying earlier, one more day and a wake up baby then I'll be back home. I can't wait to be back home with you and the kids.

"Ant I can't wait till you get home too babe." I said wiping the sweat from my forehead.

Meanwhile

"Why have you been ignoring my calls Ciara? I shouldn't have to fly here to gain your attention. You're my wife and you should act like it." Kanye demanded.

"Wife?" I chuckled. "I was your wife too when you were busy fucking that whore in our pool. Don't you come here and pull your wife card out on me!" I yelled.

"How could you serve me with divorce papers while you're out of town? I thought that we were going to work things out and go to counseling? Ciara I love you, it was the biggest mistake that I've made." Kanye said hugging me.

I pushed him off of me. "You damn right that was the biggest mistake that you ever made. Look what your mistress emailed me." I pulled out my cell phone to pull up my emails. This was something that I didn't tell anyone and that sealed the deal for me to divorce Kanye. His white whore sent me all the emails of her and Kanye discussions. It was heartbreaking to read them but I did it anyway. "Look what your Petty Becky sent me yesterday."

Kanye read some of the emails, by the look of his eyes he realized that it was the emails between him and his lover. "Fuck her Ciara, she's just upset because I cut her completely off."

"You told her that you were going to leave me earlier this month. But, you couldn't because my mother died, so you told her to wait till after everything settled down. Damn, you better blessed that you're still alive mother fucker!" I cried.

Kanye was speechless, he knew that he fucked up. He better just take this divorce and get the fuck on. At this point nothing he could say or do to get my heart back. The love that I once had for Kayne was dead. He could have all of that shit that he ever bought me, I don't want it. I have my own damn money, I'll get my own shit.

"So it's going to end like this Ciara? I can't do anything to have you back at home with me?"

"No Kanye, it's over. May you please leave now? I have to put the children to bed." I said

"Can I at least see Kenya?" Kanye asked.

"Sure you can see your daughter. She's upstairs watching television." I said.

I allowed him to see Kenya for a while. Kenya was happy to see her father, before he left she cried for him. It hurt me inside to see my baby cry for her father. Kanye also said goodbye to Eric Jr. After Kanye left I just sat in silence crying.

The next day was the model call for the fashion show. Although we had only one week to announce the model call, the turnout was great. We had eighty one models lined up out the door. With the help of my two gay male friends, Greg and Percy, we had to choose twenty models for the show. London conducting the models, she took their comp cards and gave them a number to wear as they tried out for us. I was amazed by all the beautiful women that showed up. They were all shapes, shades and sizes.

"Finally, we have our twenty models. Did we make a good choice? I said with their photos in front of me.

"It was hard but we managed to narrow it down to the best twenty in our eyes." Percy said.

"Girl, I felt like I was in LA. Call the girls in, I'm anxious to tell them the good news." Greg happily said.

London call the twenty models that we chose back inside. They nervously walked back inside prepared to hear the news.

"Congratulations ladies I'm Ciara the owner and I will love for you to model for, Bella Boutiques Summer Fashion Show. London is going to give you paperwork to fill out. The paperwork contains your contract, it has your rehearsal time and please be at every rehearsal. At the end of the fashion show you will be presented with a check and a free signature piece from Bella's. Thank you for bringing it ladies, now let's represent for Chicago!" I happily said.

"Yasssss ladies! Show them what Chicago got." Greg and Percy snapped their fingers.

"Ladies this is Greg and Percy, they will show you how to walk, tell you what to wear, pretty much you will see them more than me. Do anyone have any questions?" I asked. No one said anything. "Okay I'll let you go over your paperwork ladies."

The hard part was over with, now we had to get to work. I noticed that Alicia was missing in the group of girls. "London, where is Alicia?" I asked.

"She stepped outside." London replied.

I took a step out of the door to go get Alicia. I needed to get her fitted right away for a custom piece that I needed immediately. When I stepped outside, Alicia was in the middle of having a conversation with an older woman. The woman looked like the streets have gotten the best of her. Alicia and the woman was going back and forth about something. When Alicia tried to walk away the woman chased after her. Alicia went into her pocket to give her some money. Enough of watching the altercation, I intervened.

"Alicia honey, here you are. I was looking for you, I need you for a fitting." I walked over and said.

"Oh Ciara, I was just talking to my mom. I'll be there in a second." Alicia said with her head held down.

"Hello, I'm Alicia's mother, Samantha." The woman extended her hand out for me to shake. She reeked of alcohol. I shook her hand.

"Hey I'm Ciara, your daughter Alicia is a very beautiful and talented young lady. You should be very proud of her." I said shaking her hand.

"That's my baby. I knew from the moment when she was born that she was going to be a star. Do you have some money? I hope that you're paying my daughter pretty well." Samantha said.

"Ma! That's enough!" Alicia yelled, shoving her mother away. Her mother didn't seemed to think that she said anything wrong.

"Take your time, I'll be inside waiting on you inside Alicia." I walked away leaving Alicia alone with her mom.

I was very familiar with Alicia's situation. When I looked at her mother, all I saw was my mom, Brenda. That poor girl Alicia had her hands full. My heart went out to her right now. I walked into the bathroom and splashed water on my face. "Ok God, I know that you sent this young girl my way to help her." I said to myself in the mirror. It was such a coincidence and I believed that God will use you in order to help others. It was a knock on the door. "Just a second, I'll be right out." I yelled. The person on the other side of the door didn't say anything. I tried my hands off and stepped out. Alicia was standing outside the door crying.

"I apologize for my mother behavior Ciara." She cried.

"Step into my office Alicia." We both walked inside my old office, sitting down on the lounge. "Alicia you don't have to apologize for your mother behavior."

"She's always embarrassing me. Showing up drunk and acting out. You have no idea how I feel right now." Alicia said.

"Oh yes I do. I used to be you when I was younger. How long has she been drinking?" I asked.

"She's been drinking since I was five years old. It all started when my father was killed in a car accident. I was only five years old, but I remembered everything like it was yesterday. We were a happy family till my father's death. Samantha started off drinking wine to drinking hard liquor. By the age of six, she was deep into it. My aunts raised me from the age of twelve when they found out that she was having a different man around me every day just to get her wasted and to pay the bills. Her I am now, nineteen years old and she's out here bad. Ciara she lives in a shelter, I refuse to let her know where I live. Bobby and I have a cozy one bedroom apartment in Forest Park. I love her but I can't allow her to damage my future. It's best if I love her from a distance." Alicia said.

"I understand totally where you are coming from. I tell you what, one day next week I will like to spend some time with you. I will try my best to get some help for your mom. She still has a chance as long as she has breath in her body.

Sweetie dry your eyes and clean your face. I got your back, now give me hug."

Alicia and I both hugged before going back out. The rest of the day I managed to get a lot accomplished. I was looking forward to my fashion show.

Chapter Twelve

Sitting parked inside my car I watched several women line up outside of Ciara's boutique. When two women walked by, I politely asked them what was going on.

"There is a model call being held for a fashion show." They both said.

Ciara was planning a fashion show for her new line of lingerie and swimwear. I find it mighty strange how we both had the same concept in mind. When I went to Smooth with the idea and asked him for the money he didn't want to help me out. Now all of a sudden Miss Ciara strolls into town, back with Smooth and poof....doing my idea. I swear before fucking God. I hate Smooth so damn much right now. What does this bitch Ciara have between her legs, magic pussy or something? This bitch make me want to kill her, if I had the cash I'll put a hit on her. Right now my world was spiraling out of control. I was thinking heavily about closing down my shoe boutique. Wasn't nobody buying shoes like that, I don't know what the hell I was thinking about doing when I opened up that bullshit. It was not too late to make a change in plans and to start a new business. Tired of sitting out front stalking Ciara, I pulled off heading home. I realized that I could be working on improving myself instead of trying to compete with her. As I cruised down Madison, Smooth hit my line demanding to see me. To my surprise he invited me to his place. I jumped on the opportunity, happy to hear from him.

Smooth was sitting on his couch comfortably, it had been such a very long time since I've been to his place. I thought that the two of were alone but, our daughter Variyah was there. She was watching cartoons and playing with her dolls.

"Mama, I miss you." Variyah jumped into my arms giving me a big hug.

"I miss my baby girl so much." I smothered her with kisses as she giggled trying to get away from me.

Variyah sat back down at her table and continued to watch cartoons. "What's up Smooth, what do you want to talk about?" I asked him.

"I called you here to discuss you signing over your parental rights to me. After witnessing drugs in your premises I don't want my daughter living with you." Smooth said.

"Oh I see, so you want me to just give our daughter to you. Just like that, nah Smooth it don't work like that. What we're doing right now is perfectly fine." I said.

"No it's not, it's unacceptable for you to just pop up to my mother's house whenever you fill like it. You broke the rules Kayla, you know that you aren't allowed over my mother's home without my permission. We can do it this way or we can get the court involved." Smooth threaten me.

Ha! Ha! Ha! "Smooth you don't want to get the court involved. First of all your past isn't squeaky clean Mr. Let's not forget about your background, do you remember our domestic disputes. Plus your mother is too damn old to be raising Variyah. Doesn't she have high blood pressure and diabetes? Unhealthy, hmmm that won't hold up in court. So what, I get high for recreational activities. You may have had a good case against Erica's mother but, you don't have a good case with me. I could stop getting high right now, pass the drug test and you will lose. But, signing over my parental rights could be arranged for a small price." I said.

Smooth was pissed off because he knew that everything that I said was right. I also knew that he was willing to do whatever when it came to his children. "I'm not surprised that you want to get paid. What do you want Kayla?" he asked through clenched teeth.

"Fifty thousand, you got it. I need it for my new business. You give me that, you can have full custody of our daughter, with four visitations out of the month. Deal or no deal?"

Smooth looked into my eyes, they were filled with hate. At this moment I didn't care how he or his damn mama felt about me. I was entitled to a lot of things simply because I put up with this nigga shit for years.

"Deal, Kayla all you care about is money. Tomorrow I will get the form from the clerk of court. Then I will have my lawyer write the agreement and we'll have to get it notarized. After that we have to get the judge approval."

"Money makes the world go round baby. First I want the money, you can Chase quick pay me. After that we can do whatever it is that you're talking about. Are we done here?" I asked.

"Yes we are. Kayla if you're not busy, maybe you should spend some time with Variyah right now. My mom said that she was screaming for your last night in her sleep." Smooth said.

"Really, I mean if that's cool with you then I don't mind." Smooth gave me the okay to stay a little longer at his place with Variyah. She wanted to watch movies and order pizza. She demanded t have both of her parents involvement. Smooth and I got along for the few hours while I was there. We watched cartoon after cartoon as Variyah explained to us who her favorite animated character was and who was who. Variyah was such a very smart girl to be five years old. She told us that she wanted to earn Spanish and to play the piano. Smooth pulled out his IPad and began searching for lessons. I lucked up when I got pregnant by him, he was a great father. I on the other hand was a horrible mom. I can admit that I am, it's only because I never was shown what a good mother was. Deep down inside I never wanted to have children, ever. If I would've been free when I found out that I was pregnant with Variyah, she would not have been here today. Signing over my parental rights was easy for me. Being a part time mom will allow me to still live my life. Smooth's phone rang, it was Ciara calling him. Her face popped up on his phone screen, his sprung ass. I became jealous instantly as he talked to her on the phone. When a funny cartoon scene came on, I laughed extra loudly on purpose just to make sure Ciara could hear in me in the background. It must've worked because Smooth walked off into the back of his house.

"Yes that's Kayla, I'm allowing her to spend some time with Variyah at my home." I said.

"Oh that's sweet of you, tell me the truth Smooth. Have she tried to fuck you yet?" Ciara asked me with an attitude.

"Actually no, you know that I've never sleep with Kayla again. We both discussed about signing over her parental rights with me. She agreed to it for a small price." I said.

"Smooth I'm not shocked to hear that. Once a gold digging whore, always a gold digging whore. Make sure to get everything in writing so the bitch can't say shit. You know what, enough about her. My day was very productive, I managed to get my models for my fashion show. Everything is working out just fine on my end. What time will I see you tonight?" Ciara said.

"Around seven pm, do you mind coming by here instead?" I asked.

"No I don't mind at all, that's actually better. After I drop the children off to your mom, I'll be by there. See you later and you better not have any form of sexual relations with Kayla. Smooth, I'm learning to trust you all over again." Ciara warned me.

"Look baby it's all about me and you. I love you and see you tonight." I said.

"I love you more." Ciara said.

When I stepped back in the front Variyah and Kayla was gone. Quickly I panicked and ran out the front door. Kayla's car was still parked out front so I went back inside my house. "Variyah where are you?" I yelled out for her name. There was no answer, I searched every bedroom. When I made it to my third bedroom they were inside. Kayla had put Variyah to bed, she was rubbing her forehead.

"Oh I thought that you ran off with her." I said.

"No, why would I do that? She was sleeping so I laid her down while you were talking to that bitch Ciara. My time is up, I'll be back in touch with you soon. Don't forget about our deal that we discussed." Kayla seen herself out the door.

Getting here fifty thousand wasn't a problem. I had that amount and more put away at my mother's house. Kayla was being too nice, she had to have something up here sleeve. I didn't trust her shady ass. If I could get away with killing her, she would've been dead a very long time ago. But, I thought about Variyah, thought about how much she loved her mom. Variyah didn't see no wrong in her mother, she was crazy about her. I didn't want to see my daughter hurt like Erica was when her mother Rochelle died. Still to this day Erica has a problem with the death of her mother. She has nightmares about the shooting. Erica has received at home counseling for many years due to that incident.

I made sure that all of my doors were locked before I relaxed to watch ESPN. Watching the scores were more important because I had a lot of money on the games. Red, Vell, Ant and I always bet on the games. So far I was losing to them all. Ant was one lucky guy, he was busy taking all of our money while he was locked up. I drifted off to sleep while watching baseball. Variyah tapped me on the shoulder.

"Daddy, daddy wake up. Your phone is ringing." She said.

"Yes baby I'm up. I picked up my phone. "Hello, yes Dr. Willis, I dozed off, no it's fine I can talk." I said.

"Eric I have some great news. All your test results came back fine. We can schedule your surgery for next week. If that's fine with you." Dr. Willis said.

"Great, let's do it as soon as possible Dr. Willis. I prefer the earliest appointment so I can get it over with." I said.

Dr. Willis transferred me to his receptionist so that I can make an appointment for more vasectomy reversal. I was scheduled for surgery next week on Monday. My buddies thought I was crazy for doing what I was doing. It was my life and I really didn't care what they thought. Money wasn't a problem, I could afford another child. Variyah starting whining for her grandmother.

"Daddy I'm ready to go back to grandma house."

"Okay baby let's get ready to go. Did you enjoy yourself today?" I asked her.

"Yes I like coming over your house. I wish that all of us could live together."

"Who is all of us?" I asked Variyah, she was very mature for her age.

"Me, you, Erica, and my brother Eric. All of us." She said.

"One day it will happen baby girl. How do you feel about Ciara? Do you like her?" I asked wanting to see how she felt.

"I like Ciara, she's pretty and nice." Variyah said.

I smiled when I heard that she liked Ciara. I had plans on making Variyah's wish come true really soon. I've been retired since the age of thirty three. Now being the age of thirty five it was time for me to raise my family. Kayla did make a good point about my mother becoming too old to raise my children. As I drove to my mother's place I thought about the good times that Ciara and I had when we were a family. Now with Ciara and Kanye divorcing things could get back to the way things used to be. I can move my family out of Chicago for good, go down south and live like a King and Queen.

Chapter Thirteen

This morning Ant was scheduled to be in court. I didn't bother to send the children to child care, we all went to court instead. Everyone was there to support Ant, me, Ciara, Marilyn and Shawn. Smooth, Vell and Red haven't arrived yet, they weren't never on time for shit. Before court began, I was able to talk to Bliss shortly. After speaking with him I was ready to get everything done and over with. Court started on time, the judge came out and we all stood up to honor him. Ant case was called first. Ant came out dressed up, but was still shackled down. It didn't take long for the judge to take a look at his case. Bliss spoke and so did the defense, moments later the judge announced that Ant was not guilty. He was to be released within the next twenty four hours. When the judge said not guilty I was fucking happy.

Standing outside, I waited patiently for Ant to walk out the federal prison doors. Ant walked out around six in the evening. We stood face to face for an only a second. I jumped into his arms kissing him. Tears fell down my face, I loved Ant so damn much. We didn't say a word, just looked into each other eyes. Our silence was golden and spoke in volumes. The love that Ant and I shared was indescribable. We've been through a lot, broke days, crazy bitches, kidnappings, death, grinding, getting money, starting businesses, marriage, having children, prison and no matter what we were there for each other. Never leaving each other side, Ant was my first and only love, my true love. I'll do whatever for my man, because I know that he would do it twice if he had to for me. I can't ever imagine my life without him. The drive home was all laughs as I shared with him the moments that he missed while he was locked up. I never told him about his mother surgery or her and Shawn sleeping together. I was looking forward to his reaction once he seen Marilyn and what happened between Shawn and Marilyn would be our secret.

"Surprise!" Everyone yelled when Ant and I walked through the door. He was so happy to be surrounded by his family and friends. Jasmine and Justin jumped into their father arms. "Daddy we miss you." Ant smothered them with kisses. "I miss my babies too, did you drive your mommy crazy while I was gone?" Ant asked them.

"No we were good." They both said laughing.

Everyone gave him hugs, the last person to give him a hug was Marilyn. "Hey son, it's me your mother. Come and give me a hug." Marilyn said.

"Mom, you look different." Ant said as he hugged her.

"I got a little work done son. Anyway, I'm happy that you're finally home." Marilyn said.

Pulling Ant away from his mom, I steered him off into the dining room. The table was set with his soul food fest that he asked for. You know that I didn't cook, I had the food catered from Priscilla's Ultimate Soul food. It was a thanksgiving in June, everyone pulled up a seat prepared to eat. I led us off into prayer. You know I learned how to pray from the best, GG. I kept it short because everyone was ready to eat and so was I. Honestly I wanted to skip this part, put everyone out and make love to my man. I wasn't going to be selfish with Ant, I know that I wasn't the only person who missed him. We all ate, joked and laughed, after dinner the men went down the basement to talk. All the ladies stayed upstairs to gossip and help me clean up. It didn't take long for Aaliyah, Denise and Ciara to question me.

"So what do you plan on doing special for him tonight? Whatever it is I just hope that you don't get pregnant." Ciara laughed as she joked.

"I have some sexy lingerie. Do yawl remember the time when Tia taught me those pole lessons and I tried to do it for Ant? That shit was an epic fail." I laughed so damn hard.

"Yes, that was super funny. You had bruises all over your body from the carpet burns when you hit the floor." Denise laughed.

"I didn't really have anything planned. It's just going to be raw and uncut, that's the best." I said.

Tonight was going to special without all the side effects. I was letting my guard down, no condoms and yes I still made my husband wear condoms. I wasn't on birth control so to prevent from getting pregnant, I made Ant wear a condom or pull out. Tonight I didn't mind if he went raw or didn't pull out. I was down for whatever. If he wanted to pop a pill, I was popping one with him. Tonight we were both going to be rolling.

We all had to holler at Ant about the business deal that went down. He was excited to hear about making more money. I put up his half, only because I knew that he would pay me back.

"Man that's what's up. I'm getting out making more money. Where the weed at Red? Fire that shit up." Ant said. Vell pulled out the zip locked bag of weed and swishers. He rolled up the blunt while they sat at the table discussing their next move. Moments later Ant was inhaling some good shit. An hour went by before everyone gathered to leave. Kelly waited for Ant upstairs alone in their bedroom, wearing her canary yellow lingerie set. She sat at the vanity applying her makeup, which was flawless.

"Perfect." I sprayed some Flower Bomb over my body.

Ant stepped inside admiring my beauty. He hugged me from behind, "I want to say thank you for always being there for me. You've always been my light at the end of the tunnel. I'm grateful to have you in my life. You and the children mean everything to me. I love you so much." Ant started to cry.

I turned around to face him. "Since the first day we became serious, I told you that it was me and you against world. It was hard giving my heart to someone but, I trusted you with mine. You taught me how to love and I'm happy that I let my guard down. I love you Ant and no one can come between that, ever."

We kissed one another as our children twisted the door knob. In walks Jasmine and Justin with their pajamas on. Ant and I laughed, we couldn't put them out. Covering up my body, I threw on my satin canary yellow robe.

"Mommy, daddy can we sleep with you tonight?" Jasmine and Justin begged.

"Sure you can." Ant said.

He was always spoiling them and giving them their way. I was ready to make love, hell it's a long time since I've had some of Ant. I went to change into something more appropriate and so did Ant. We all gathered into our California King sized bed. When I tried to lie my head on Ant's chest, Jasmine shoved me out of the way. "Momma move over some, you taking up all the room." Jasmine whined. I moved over as Ant laughed at his two favorite girls fighting over him. Justin was already sleep on the other end of the bed. It was enough room for me so I snuggled up next to him and fell asleep.

In the middle of the night I tossed and turned, not being able to get much sleep at all. Looking at the time on my phone it was two am. I made my way downstairs to get a glass of water. My mouth was dry, my body was drenched with night sweats. Everyone was still sleeping, the house was very quiet. So much was on my mind causing me to not rest. I didn't want to disturb Ant out of his sleep, he deserved to have a good night rest after spending three weeks in jail. My mother was on mind, maybe it was time for me to go visit her. I had a nightmare that she was released but didn't want to see me or my children because I cut her off. That bothered me because I loved my mother very much. As I sat at my dining room table sipping on the glass of water I went into a deep trance. Jas appeared it the sit across from me. She was beautiful, her radiant brown skin glowed just like it did seven years ago.

"Jas, I miss you so much Sis. I'm so glad that you came to see me, it's been such a very long time since we've talked." I said.

"True, don't worry about me Kelly. I'm always watching over you and Ciara all the time. What's going on with you? Why aren't you upstairs with your family?" Jas asked.

"Girl I can't sleep, I keep thinking about my mom. I haven't been to see her in over year and that's not right. At night when I dream, she always appear in them even when she doesn't have anything to do with them." I explained.

"Hmmm, I understand. The dreams are telling you to spend time with your mom. Kelly she's all that you and Shawn have. She may have been removed from society, but she doesn't have to be removed from your life. You shouldn't treat her any different just because she's incarcerated. Please go and see your mom." Jas said.

"You're right, I'm going to go visit her this weekend. I miss her so much." I cried.

"No need to cry Kelly. I love you and make sure you kiss them babies for me." Jas disappeared. Marilyn walked downstairs in the kitchen. She turned on the light and jumped when she noticed me sitting at the table in the dark.

She grabbed her chest," Shit Kelly you scared me, what are you doing sitting in the dark?" Marilyn asked.

"I couldn't sleep so I came down here. The children are in the bed with us tonight." I said.

"I told them not to go in there. They smart asses waited till I went to sleep to creep out the bedroom." Marilyn laughed.

"It's fine, they miss their father just as much as me. Well I'm going back upstairs to get some sleep. Marilyn if you keep on eating late at night like this, you're going to pick back up that weight you loss." I warned Marilyn as she filled her bowl with butter pecan ice-cream.

When I made it back to my room Ant was lying in the bed alone. Yes, he put the children in their own beds. I crept in the bed and pounced on top of him. He looked into my eyes, I knew what time that it was. It didn't take long for us to get naked. His rock hard dick entered deep inside of me. I had to catch my breath, it's been a while for me. I was used to getting dick down every day. Ant grabbed my hips as I kissed him on the side of his neck.

"I don't think that I could hold it in much longer. Damn! Shit!" Ant moaned.

As I bounced up and down on his dick I was close to my climax. My eyes rolled to the back of head. I tried my best not to scream and wake up the children. Ant came first, he filled me upside. I wasn't done yet, I continued to ride his semi limp dick until I came all over it. He felt so good inside of me that I didn't want to hop off of it.

"Sorry babe for busting to fast, you put that good pussy on me like that. It was built up inside of me, that's why I kicked the kids out of the bed." Ant laughed.

"We're not finished yet." I went down licking cum off of his dick, slurping and spitting on it. His dick rose back up but I didn't stop deep throating him. Ant forced his dick down my throat causing me to gag. I swallowed up the nut as he came twice for the night. After that I sat on his face feeding him my sweet pussy.

Chapter Fourteen

Red came with me to have my surgery done. He tried to talk me out of it, but I wasn't trying to hear shit that he was saying. The nurse took my vital signs and prep me for surgery. Dr. Willis went over the surgery, telling me what to expect after wards. I'm not going to lie, I became nervous when they had me signing beneficiary paperwork. All I thought about was when Brenda went in to have surgery and died on the exam table. After I was finished filling out the paperwork, they were ready to begin.

"Eric were going to put you to sleep by placing the mask on your face. Count to ten for us." Dr. Bliss instructed.

"One, two, three." By the time that I counted to four I was asleep.

The surgery was over in two hours. I was feeling a little pain in my groin. Dr. Willis told me not to worry and gave me something for pain. They me pushed off to recovery unit to monitor my vitals. Red was waiting on me patiently, he was too busy checking on the scores from off his app on the phone.

"You good Smooth, how to feel right now?" He asked me laughing.

"I feel like a man again." I joked. "Shit I'm ready to make me another boy."

Dr. Willis came walking inside laughing, he overheard the conversation between me and Red. "Not so fast Eric. You won't be able to have sex for another two weeks. Some patients recover faster than others. So I say a week give or take." He explained.

He handed me my after surgery papers advising me to read over them. I thanked him for turning back into a man again. He assured me that I was able to produce children for the next twenty years. Red just shook his head, still not believing that I underwent the surgery. If everything was fine with me, I would be released in the morning. I couldn't eat anything, they made me NPO. Red make sure that I was straight before he left.

"Aye, make sure that you call me to let me know what's going on." We shook up.

"Alright player, I'll call you when I'm ready." I said.

Meanwhile

While I was driving on my way to meet my lawyer, I received a phone call. It was Kanye's mom, Cathy calling me. I thought to myself, wow this grown ass man sent his momma on me. I prepared myself for this fucking phone call. As soon as I picked up the phone she gave me her deepest condolences for the loss of my mother. I thanked her even though she didn't bother to call me when it happened. You see Kanye's parents were uppity rich black folks. Cathy was snotty and his father Kenneth, didn't really care about much. He just provided the money and played golf while Cathy went shopping and to the boat. She went on and on about how her son was feeling. I gave her the floor, allowing her to talk. As I listened to her talk about something that she had no knowledge of, Kanye fell to tell her the truth.

"Cathy I'm going to say this, your Kanye isn't innocent. As a matter of fact did he tell you that he was having an affair? Did he tell you that I caught him having sex with his mistress in our family pool? Did he tell you that he planned on leaving me? No, I don't think that he did. I will appreciate it if you stay out of your son business. Nothing you say or he say is going to make me have a change of heart." I said,

"Well Ciara if everything that you saying is true, I'm more than sure that he can get some type of help. So what he cheating on you, Kenneth cheated on me plenty of times. You know what the problem is with you young people? You're always running instead of fighting. If you loved my son you would forgive him and try to work on repairing your marriage." Cathy said.

It took all the good in me to stop from cursing his ignorant ass momma out. I counted to five before I spoke. "You know what Cathy, I don't think that you understand where I'm coming from or how I feel. Kanye hurt me deeply, he betrayed me. I don't have enough strength in my body to fight for my marriage."

Cathy tried to talk while I was talking. I didn't want to hear shit what she was talking about so I hung up the phone on her ass. She called me back several times, but I didn't answer. I turned up the music when Beyoncé came on. Right now I didn't have time for Kanye or his damn mom. Before I stepped inside the building, I adjusted my attitude.

"Hello I'm Ciara Robinson, here to see Mr. Einkorn." I said politely to the secretary at the front desk.

"Good morning Ciara, Mr. Einkorn is waiting for. Please follow me to his office."

I followed the woman to Mr. Einkorn office, he was on the phone talking. I took a seat, "Would you like anything to drink?" His secretary asked me.

"No I'm fine, thank you." I said.

Mr. Einkorn ended his phone call, giving me his attention. "Ciara how are you my dear?'

"I'm doing fine, taking it one day at a time." I said.

"That's good to hear. I have some good news, the hospital has agreed to offer you one hundred and fifty thousand for the accidental death of your mother. I know that the money wouldn't bring your mother back, but this is a great offer. What do you think?" Mr. Einkorn asked me.

"I'm fine with it, I'm just ready to get this phase of my life over with. It's not about the money to me, where do I sign." I said.

Mr. Einkorn presented me with paperwork. I signed my signature of several papers. "Thank you, are we done here?" I asked.

"Yes we are, you will be receiving your check tomorrow. Would you like for me to come by your home to bring it to you?"

"Yes that would be fine. I'll see you tomorrow afternoon. Thank you for everything." I left out.

When I got inside of the car I started to cry. The only person who I thought to call was Smooth. He answered quickly.

"Smooth, where are you? It's finally over, I settled with the hospital." I cried into the phone.

"I'm in the hospital right now getting my stitches removed. Do you need anything right now? I can send Red or Vell if you need me to." Smooth said.

"No I'm fine, I just had a moment. I'm on my way to the boutique right now. Call me as soon as you're done. I love you Smooth." I said.

"I love you too beautiful." Smooth said.

Grabbing a piece of tissue from out of my purse, I cleaned my face. Before I pulled off I said a prayer to God and headed to the boutique.

Back At The Hospital

Hearing Ciara cry and down made me feel bad. I wish that I could be there for her, but right now I can't. Regretting that I even lied to her in the first place, I picked up my phone to call Red. He answered and asked him to go and see about Ciara. Red knew what to do already, he was like a brother to Ciara and didn't mind being there for her. I told him to pick up some flowers and a Chanel bag.

"How in the hell do you expect me to pick out a purse for a woman? I don't nothing about purses or shoes." Red said.

"Ask the sales woman at the store. She should be able to help you out. Run downtown for me real quick, you aren't doing shit else." I said.

"Damn you owe me man. I'll call you when I get up there." Red said.

"Cool."

The nurse walked in to check on vitals. She was a young black nurse, she smiled flirting with her eyes. I knew that she was trying to give me the pussy because she had been in my room too many times. She took a look at my groin area, removing the gauze and changing them to clean ones.

"The bleeding is slowing down. You have a little bit of swelling, how do you feel? Do you have any pain?" The nurse asked.

"Just a little, can I have something for my pain."

"Yes, give me a second. I'll be right back." The nurse said.

When she left to go get my pain medicine, Red hit me up on facetime. He made it to Sak's and was talking to a sales woman about the hottest bag. She directed him to some purses and showed him a few.

"Which one you want me to grab her bro?" Red asked.

"The red one is nice." I said. The nurse walked into my room with my pain medicine. I asked her opinion on which purse that I should choose.

"Excuse me which purse do you like? I'm getting it for my woman."

"The red one is really nice." She smiled and said. I choose the red one and told Red to grab some red roses to match. We ended the phone call and I took my pain medicine.

"Your woman is very lucky to have you." The nurse said as she flirted.

"No, I'm blessed to have her. I love that woman so damn much." I smiled.

The nurse walked out of the room smiling sliding me her phone number. She reminded me of Rochelle, Erica's mom. I can see how easy it was for a doctor to be seduced by a nurse. The new nurses were very attractive, young and shaped up nicely. Nothing like the old nurses that took care of us back then. She was alright, but she wasn't Ciara. I ripped her number up and threw it away in the trash. My player days were over with now, it was time for me to grow old with one woman. Ciara was back in life and I promise this time I wasn't going to lose her.

I was busy measuring one the models preparing her for a fitting, when in walks Red. He was carrying a Sak's Fifth Avenue bag and some flowers. Smiling because I already knew that Smooth sent him my way. Red walked in saying hello to everyone.

"Hey sis, how are you? I have a special delivery for you today." Red smiled and gave me a kiss on the cheek as he handed me my treats.

"I was sad, but now I'm doing much better. Thank you Red, Smooth is crazy. He didn't have to send you." I smiled and said.

Everyone watched as I pulled out my new red Chanel purse. It was cute and really nice. The red long stem roses were beautiful. I gave Red a hug, thanking him for going out of his way. "Wait I have something that I want you to give to Denise." I went in the back quickly to get her the lingerie piece that she really loved in her size. I had Alicia wrap it up and place it inside one of our signature gift boxes. "This is something special for Denise, that I know that you will enjoy." I said giving Red the box. "Promise me that you won't open it up."

"I promise sis, alright let me get out of here. I'll see you soon Ciara, bye to everyone." Red said leaving.

I called Smooth to thank him. He seems to always amaze me every time. Funny how my day starting off in a bad way and he managed to turn it all around. As the day went on, I had selected what models would be wearing what and also have been promoting the fashion show on social media. The models rehearsed today with Greg and Percy. I was glad that I was there because I made a few changes that needed to be made. My business was growing and tickets for the fashion show was selling fast on Eventbrite. With all the bad things happening in my life, I felt that my life was crashing. With the death of my mother and a failed marriage, I still had things to be happy about. You know what that say, "New beginnings are often disguised as painful endings."

When I made it home, I spent some time with Eric Jr. and Kenya. Tomorrow I decided that I will work from home promoting my fashion show. The children and I made dinner and baked chocolate chip cookies. When Kenya said that she didn't want to go back to Arizona and that she liked her much better I was shocked to hear that. Now was the time for me to have a talk with my children.

"Eric and Kenya momma have to tell you about some changes that are going to happen in our family. How would you like to move to Chicago permanently?" I asked them.

"Yes! Cool!" They both said. Will daddy be with us momma?" Kenya asked.

"No daddy is going to live in Arizona, but we are going to live in Chicago. Your father and I are getting a divorce. A divorce means that two people separating from marriage. Now this doesn't mean that he doesn't love you anymore.

He will still be able to be a part of your life and see you. Do you have any questions?" I asked them both.

"Yes, when will I see my daddy again?" Kenya asked.

"If you like tomorrow, he's still in town. As a matter of fact, I will call him now, would you like that?" I asked her. "Yes can I please talk to him?" Kenya requested.

Chapter Fifteen

Today the children and I arrived at Logan Correctional Center. It has been a very long time since I've been here and my children very first time. Jasmine and Justin asked me a million questions as we walked inside the prison. I signed at the front desk. The guards complimented my children and were very nice. We sat down until they called my name. When it was time to walk through the metal detectors my children questioned the guards. I laughed because they were so smart and funny. When we took a seat at the table in the waiting area, they knew who we were there to see.

"Momma are we here to see grandma? They both asked me.

"Yes we are, we're going to surprise her." I said.

"Cool we love surprises. We should've brought her a gift momma. Next time can we bring her gift when we come?"

"Yes and we can send her gift in the mail to if you like.' I told them.

Moments later my mom walked into the waiting area. When she laid eyes on us, she ran over to us quickly.

"Kelly, my grand babies, Oh my God what a surprise" she gave us all a hug.

"Grandma, momma said that you love surprises." Jasmine and Justin said hugging their grandma back. She smothered them with kisses. She looked really good, her face was full, her skin was clear and her teeth were white. She was in perfect shape and her hair was very long and braided into two French braids with a middle part.

"Mom it's so good to see you. I miss you so much and I apologize for not coming to see you." I said.

"No problem baby girl, let's put the past behind us and start from the beginning. How have you been doing, how is Anthony doing? My mother asked.

During my visit I filled her in on everything that happened within the last year. The children and I had a great time with my mother. Jasmine sat in her lap and Justin told her about his little girlfriend that he had. It was like the good old days. My mother told me all about her appeal and that she may be coming home soon. I was happy to hear that and told her that she can stay with me. When the visit was over the children and I didn't want to go. I promised my mother that we will be back in two weeks. She was fine with that, I gave her a hug and didn't want to let her go.

I called Ant so that he could help me with his sleeping children in the backseat. He met me in the garage to help me carry them inside. Marilyn undressed them and put them to bed for us. Since Ant has been home, she still continued to be a big help around the house. Ant was busy counting his money as he sat across the bed. He had every thousand sectioned off into piles.

"How was the visit with your mom? Did you tell her that I said hello?" he asked me.

"The visit was great, the kids and I had a wonderful time. My mother looks good and I'm praying that she is released soon from this appeal. I told her that she could move with us when it happens. She asked about you and said hello." I said giving Ant a kiss.

"That's good to hear, you know that she's more than welcome to stay here. This is all of today's earnings. Today I rode on the joint to hang out the crew. I treated them all to Pappadeaux's and had a good time. You know I had to show them some love. I know how it feels being out there on the block hustling." Ant said.

"That was cool of you to do. We've both have grown together. I remember those days of you rolling around in your old school on dubs. I was right by your side rapping a Twista song. "Ant and I laughed.

"You used to have me chasing your ass, sweating you. I still remember the day when you, Ciara and Jas was in the restaurant parking lot. When we all met for the first time. Damn that was a very long time ago." Ant said.

"Yes it is, Ant don't laugh. I have something to share with you. You know that we talk about everything right. Over the years when I start to worry about things, Jas will appear and talk to me. At first when it happened I was afraid, but now I'm used to." I told him.

"That's pretty normal for that to happen, especially how close that you were. Maybe you and Ciara need to go and visit her." Ant said.

"Yes, I agree. It's time that I go visit her and GG." I said. Ant and I counted fifteen thousand that night. We rolled around in the bed covered with money and made love.

This morning Mr. Einkorn dropped off my check. I went by the bank to deposit it into my account and went back in the house. Kenya has been busy bugging me about seeing her father. I called Kanye and he came by to see her. I allowed them to spend some time together, no matter how he treated me. I will never take his daughter from him as long as he doesn't turn her against me. Kanye asked if he could take Kenya out to eat and shopping.

"Thanks for letting me take her out. We will be back in a few hours." Kanye said.

"No problem just make sure that you have her back at a reasonable time. Oh and Kanye, don't have my daughter around no other woman." I warned him.

"Ciara why would I do something like that?" He asked me.

I didn't even bother to respond, I rolled my eyes and shut the door behind them. It was only Eric Jr. and I alone in the house. He helped me pack so more of my mother old things. Tomorrow the Good Will would be by to pick everything up. I wanted to throw a yard sell, but I didn't have enough time to have it over the weekend. My son was a really big help, he was taking the move back to Chicago very well. It was different for him because he had Chicago blood in his body. My plan was to live here maybe for a year and then sell my mother house. I certainly had more than enough money to live anywhere. Plus my businesses was growing, flying back and forth to all of my stores were going to be added to my business plans. Time was going by fast and we haven't had anything to eat. I was too hot for me to cook so Eric Jr, and I went to grab a bite to eat. He wanted pasta, so I took him to Olive Garden. While I was there his father called his cell phone. I could tell that it was Smooth because of the conversation. Eric Jr. handed me his phone.

"Daddy wants to talk to you mom?"

I got on the phone. "What's up Smooth? Thank you for the gift yesterday." I said.

"You're welcome, I got a little busy last night and couldn't see you. Do you mind if I come by there later on to see you and Jr?" Smooth asked.

"You know that I can't wait to see you. I'll text you when I make it home. Right now I'm spending time with my son, we're on a date. See you soon." I teased Smooth laughing. I enjoy playing with him and making him jealous.

I ended the phone call laughing at Ciara. She was being cute and trying to make me jealous. I was now at home, discharged out of the hospital. With Dr. Bliss strict instructions, the swelling should go down within a week. He made me that I wouldn't have sex until two weeks. That was a promise that I was going to break. As soon as the swelling went down, I was back to making love to Ciara. Throughout the day I had to make some runs and check up on my paper. Since Ant was back down I didn't really need to go out as much. He made sure that everything was operating at the bar and checked on the shorties who worked the block. Red had his hands full with the quads birthday party that was coming up. Vell went back home for a week, leaving his daughters with his mother. Vell and Aaliyah needed to handle some business in Atlanta. When I was able to sit down and blow one, I hit up my cousin Tommy. I haven't had a chance to rap with him about everything that was going on. Over the last five years I would travel to Texas once a year to visit my family.

"What's up cuz? What the hell you been on man? I asked Tommy when he answered.

"Damn cuz where the hell you been? I was just talking about you to Tia, she just asked about you." Tommy said.

"Oh yeah, tell Tia I said what's up. Man cuz, I've been chilling and getting money you know me. Tommy I did something that I thought that I would never do." I said.

"What's that cuz, did you get someone else pregnant. Wait, it can't be that, because you got nipped right." Tommy joked.

"Damn cuz, I didn't get anyone pregnant yet, but I plan on it."

"How in the fuck you plan on doing that Smooth?" Tommy asked.

"I got a vasectomy reversal yesterday man. That's right, I changed my mind about having more children. I want at least two more with Ciara."

"Is that even possible to make happen? I'm clueless to this type of shit. Damn I can't believe that you did it. I remember when you got your vasectomy after Ciara left you. Ciara got your ass sprung cuz." Tommy laughed and said.

"Yeah man, she got a nigga heart I'm not going to lie. She has no idea that I did it though. I plan on telling her soon. I just don't know how to break it to her."

"That's going to be tough right there. What's going on with her marriage? Her and dude must not be together anymore?" Tommy asked.

"No they aren't. Ciara filed for divorce and moving back here." I kept it short, not wanting to tell Tommy that Kanye cheating on her. "I was happy to hear that because I will be able to see Junior more."

"Well cuz, I wish you the best of luck. Tell the fellas I said what's up, but I gotta get out of here. Royalty has to get her school physical, she's starting kindergarten." Tommy said.

"Alright Tommy, I'll be up there soon to chop it up off with you. Love you cuz." I said.

"Love you to cuz, be safe out there in Chicago. I know you not worried about nothing, but keep your head up." Tommy said.

"You know me Tommy. I keep three pieces on me, they can't catch me slipping." I said.

After I got off the phone I called my mother to check on her. She was doing fine and reading her bible. She told me that she had a dream that Ciara had gotten pregnant by me. I listened to her tell me the dream, but I never told her that I had the surgery. She never knew about me having a vasectomy. I didn't want my mother all in my business when it came to that. We talked for a few minutes, Erica and Variyah were at their summer classes. I told her that I would take them both for the weekend and give her break. My mother deserved it, she was a great grandmother.

It was 6:37 pm when I made it to Ciara's place. My son greeted me at the door, I called and told him that I was pulling up. He was very excited to see me. I gave him a baseball and bat that I purchased from Walmart. We were going to play ball this weekend at the park. When I walked in Ciara was sitting on the couch. She seemed to be upset about something, a frown was on her face.

"What's wrong with you Ciara? Why are you looking mad?" I asked her.

"Kanye came by to pick up Kenya and I haven't heard from him since. He's not answering any of my calls or text messages. If I don't hear from him soon, I'm calling the police." Ciara said.

"Calm down, no need to get the police involved. If he doesn't come back with her, then you already know where he is headed. Hopefully that's not the case and he will show up with her soon." I said.

Ciara was pissed off, she paced the floor back and forth. By 7:24 pm Kanye pulled up to the house. Ciara rushed outside to meet him. They both started arguing while Kanye was carrying a sleepy Kenya. Ciara tried to take Kenya inside, but Kanye insisted on carrying her inside instead. I was getting tired of the hide from Kanye games. When Kanye yelled at Ciara and told her to get out of his way, that's when I stepped in.

"Ciara I got this, you take Kenya in the house." I walked down the stairs toward Kanye. He gave Kenya to Ciara and squared up.

"Oh that's why you want a divorce so that you can be back with your baby daddy?" Kanye laughed. "Look Smooth this has nothing to do with you, unless you want to involve yourself." Kanye lame ass said.

"When it comes to Ciara it has everything to do with me. Don't you ever disrespect her again, when you talk to her it better be at a respectful tone." I walked off and turned to go in the house.

Kanye was still standing there, "Fuck you and Ciara, I'm not about to play these games with you. You want her, you finally got her. I did you a favor by being a better father to your child. You should be thanking me."

Turning around I went to hit that hoe ass nigga out. Ciara ran down the stairs after me, but it was too late. Kanye and I were fighting, I was balled his ass up. He punched me in my stomach, the pain hit me because of the surgery. I knocked his ass out, Kanye collapsed to the ground. I continued to hit him, blood splatter everywhere. I was going to kill that nigga for disrespecting me.

Ciara was screaming and crying, grabbing me off him. My son stood on the porch watching all of it, he was the only reason why I stopped.

Chapter Sixteen

It's been such a very long time since I've been out of town, so when Aaliyah invited me to her home in Atlanta I jumped on it. Aaliyah was waiting on me outside Hartsfield-Jackson Atlanta Airport. She was leaning against her car wearing a pair of shades while I struggle with my luggage.

"Excuse me Queen Aaliyah, can I get some assistance?" I laughed as I stopped rolling my luggage.

"Girl, who in the hell told you to bring all of this bullshit anyway? You're only going to be here for a week. You packed for a damn month." Aaliyah helped me out, placing the luggage into her trunk.

I took a look at her cute Porsche truck. "Nice truck Aaliyah. What's up, what's popping down here in the A? I'm ready to get it cracking." I was ready to turn up.

"Damn cool down with your thirsty ass, hell you just got here. Put your seat belt on too. Anyway we will party later, right now we're going to drop your things off and go to the mall. "Aaliyah said.

"Okay you're in charge, I'm the visitor." I laughed and said.

It was my first time being in Atlanta, hell I'm ashamed to admit that it was my first time ever being on a plane before. When I called and hit Aaliyah up with everything that I was going through. She felt that I needed a break from it all. Aaliyah was cool, I know at first that we had our difference. Over the years I apologized and slowly Aaliyah allowed me back in her life. She hooked my place out and added her touch, she was good at interior decorating. Aaliyah has grown out of that young girl mentality and got on her shit. Secretly I admired that about her, it made me want to get on my shit as well.

Finally we made it to her home. It was very beautiful, she lived in a suburb called Smyrna. "Damn I see that you, Vell and the children are living nice." I was impressed by the size of Aaliyah home.

"Thank you, we work very hard in order to live a certain type of way." Aaliyah said.

We pulled into her two car garage, Vell other car was parked in the other space. They had a traditional style five bedroom home. Aaliyah gave me a tour of their home, I feel in love instantly with her nine foot ceiling. After the tour she took me to the guest room.

"This is where you would be staying. You have your very own bathroom. Make yourself at home for the reminder of your stay. Do you want to change clothes or you're ready to hit the town?" Aaliyah asked.

"Let me change into something more eye catching. I may get me a man up here." I laughed.

"Girl bye, you don't want no man from Atlanta. Hurry up, I'll be waiting for you down stairs." Aaliyah said.

An hour later I was ready, I changed into a body hugging maxi dress. My real hair was curly, I just brushed and sprayed it with leave in conditioner. We went to Lenox Square Mall and balled out. Even though my money wasn't as long as Aaliyah I still did me some shopping. Besides I was counting on receiving the money from Smooth. We worked up an appetite and sat down to eat.

"So what have you been up to, besides fighting with Smooth?" Aaliyah asked me.

"Well since you've asked, I also had a fight with Miss Ciara." Aaliyah looked at me with a shock look on her face. "Yes I bumped into her at the beauty shop and whopped her as." I lied and told Aaliyah. I wanted to know if she knew anything about the altercation that went down between Ciara and me."

"Really, because I didn't hear anything about you and Ciara fighting. Honestly I don't know why you are still fighting her over Smooth. Give it up girl and move on, it is other men out here that you can meet." Aaliyah said."

"They may be true and for the record, I'm over Smooth. I can still move on, but I will never be happy to see him with her. He could be with any other woman but Ciara. I hate that fucking bitch." I said.

"Kayla why hate, when you can work on improving yourself. It starts with you, so why be mad at her. And I know that you think that I'm taking up for her because Ciara and I are cool. That's not true, she's on her shit. I give props when props are due, but you can be on your shit too boo." Aaliyah said.

I sat right there quietly, allowing the words to sink in. Aaliyah was right, I had to work on being a better me. It was time for me to move on from Smooth and get my shit together. Apart of me was being too petty to give up on her. Over the years Smooth and I have been fucking and he's been looking out for me.

"Aaliyah it's so hard to get over him. You know that we have been still sleeping together for the last five years. As soon as Ciara come back, he just wants to cut the sex off and the money. That shit isn't right." I said.

"You know what, that was all up to you to change that. You were in control of being either his snack or either his meal. When Smooth got hungry, you were his snack. Something good, quick and small. Ciara is his meal, great, long lasting and big. She fills up his appetite never leaving him starving. For five years you could've been in her shoes, but you sold yourself short." Aaliyah said.

"Can we just change this subject because I'm getting upset? Fuck them, I came out here to get away from all the stress. Where is the waiter at, I need to order a drink." I said.

I signaled for the waiter to come over and ordered me some Henny straight. Aaliyah sat back and watched me guzzle it down. I fucked with her hard, but she wasn't going to blow me today. After we were finished, we went back to the house. I took a nap before we stepped out to the club. The club scene was a lot better than Chicago. Everything was much bigger and the people were laid back. Although I did run into a few people that were from the Chi at the party. I met some nice guys and mingled while Aaliyah sat down at the table. She was so busy texting Vell back and forth. I was enjoying myself, smoking weed and drinking. By the time that the party was over with, Aaliyah had to carry me out with the help of two men.

The sun shined brightly in my face as I fought to open my eyes. I woke up in a very fancy room and didn't know where I was. "Where am I?" I yelled as I crawled out of the bed. The room was spinning, making me dizzy.

Aaliyah ran inside the room. "Kaylah you're in my house, snap out of it."

"Who are you? Where am I? Get your hands off of me." I slurred as I yelled at her.

"Oh my fucking God! No!" Aaliyah screamed to me as I threw up all over her plush beige carpet. "Kayla get your ass up and go to the bathroom now!"

"Who the hell is Kayla? Please help me find my way home." I begged Aaliyah.

Aaliyah pulled out her cellphone to call an ambulance. The paramedics arrived trying to see what they could do. I tried to fight them because I didn't want to go with them. I didn't know who any of these people were. They strapped me down to the stretcher, making sure that I don't fall off. I went inside the ambulance, they closed the door and took me to the hospital.

By night time I woke up inside the hospital. Aaliyah was sitting by my bedside worried. "I'm glad to see that you're finally up. You slept the whole entire day." Aaliyah said.

"What the fuck am I doing in the hospital?" I asked.

"The doctor said that you wouldn't remember anything. Last night those men that you were partying with drugged you. Your blood work came back and they found Rohypnol in your system. Kayla they also found cocaine in your system. What's up with that?" Aaliyah asked

At this moment I was so embarrassed. How could I tell Aaliyah that I use coke to have fun? I turned red, I was ashamed. Instead of answering her, I turned my back on her.

"Kayla when we get back to my place, I want you to pack your shit and come home." Aaliyah was mad, she got up walking out of the hospital room.

The ride back to Aaliyah place was pure silence. I was just ready to go home and get out of her face. I went to the room to pack my belongings. Aaliyah wasn't letting me off that easy, she came in the room giving me a lecture.

"Kaylah you're too damn grown to be doing foolish bullshit. Why are you getting high? You should know fucking better! How long have this been going on? Do you know that you could've fucked yourself up from that drug combination with alcohol? It's a blessing that you're in your right state of mind right now. Girl you need to get you some help when you get back home." Aaliyah said.

"Look I'm sorry that I fucked up your carpet. I'll pay to have it cleaned." I said.

"Fuck that carpet, I'll take care of that. I'm talking about you getting clean. I can't help you if you don't want it. I'm begging you to stop now because the path that you're going down only leads to self-destruction."

"I'm a failure, everything is failing. Coke makes me feel better. I just don't want to talk about it right now!" I balled up on the floor crying.

Aaliyah hugged me. "It's going to be fine. I will check you into rehab if you like here. No one has to know Kayla."

194

"No I just want to go home."

I finished packing my things and got dressed for the airport. My flight didn't leave for another four hours, but I left for the airport anyway. Not wanting to bother Aaliyah any more, I took an Uber to the airport. Aaliyah gave me a hug before I got inside the car. I waved goodbye as the driver pulled off.

Afterwards

Damn I know that I promised Kayla that I wouldn't tell anyone what happened, but I had to tell Smooth. Vell was aware that Kayla was here, I didn't get the chance to tell him what went down. I called him first explaining the incident to him. Vell felt that I should tell Smooth simply because they shared a daughter together. I called Smooth and told him everything that happened. Smooth was very angry and upset, he also told me that he knew that she was getting high.

"Smooth please keep this between you and I that I told you. I just want Kayla to get some help. I'm not trying to talk about her, but someone else needed to know. You are the only person that close to her because she doesn't have any family."

"I won't tell anyone Aaliyah. When she get back in town, I'll go by to check on her." Smooth said.

"Smooth please take it easy on her. She's already blaming you for everything." I told him

"That's Kayla problem, she wants to place the blame everybody but herself." Smooth said before ending the call.

Chapter Seventeen

Today was the big day, Bella Boutique's Fashion Show. The place was packed and my models were ready. I was very nervous about everything. My models makeup and hair was on point and they looked beautiful in the items that I had costumed made. The show was ready to start, the lights were dimmed and my special performers came out to put on a show. I hired some dancers that were wearing costumes that glowed in the dark. The crowd went crazy as the danced to Rhianna's song Work. While they were dancing we were in the back preparing for the show. I said a small prayer before the main show. The crowd was clapping, going crazy for my performers.

"Okay ladies its show time?!" I said.

London was our MC and she introduced my models. The music played and my first model, Alicia walked out on the runway wearing a red lingerie set and heels. Alicia's mother cheered her on from the crowd and so did the other guest. One by one each model walked down the runway. My team was doing great in the back with wardrobe changes. Each model was going to walk the runway four times. Everything was going great, I peeped out into the crowd and saw Smooth and the fellas standing from a far. Smooth was frowned up and staring at someone. I took a look at what he was staring at and rolled my eyes. London walked up to me to discuss the show.

"Ciara everything is going great. We have fifteen minutes to go before you walk out." London said, but I ignored her. "What's wrong Ciara?"

"Look, how did Kayla get in here? She has to go now!" I said.

London took a look at Kayla. "Damn, she must've came in when the lights were dimmed. You know I have no problem with putting her out." London said with a bougie girl attitude.

"Wait, it looks like Smooth is handling it." We both looked over at Kaylah. Red was whispering something in her ear. Kayla got up and stormed out of the fashion show upset. Smooth and Red went outside shortly after her.

"She better be lucky that Smooth got to her ass before I did." London said.

London was something else, she always wanted the pleasure to check Kayla's ass for any reason.

Outside

"Where the fuck would you bring your dumb ass here Kayla?" I was pissed off, he didn't want to continue to be disrespectful to the mother of my daughter, but Kayla was asking for it.

"The last time I checked I was entitled to go where ever the fuck I want. You're not the boss of me Smooth." Kayla yelled.

You weren't invited, you came to start some bullshit. Gone on with that bullshit Kayla before you get hurt." I warned her.

Kayla walked off to her car getting inside. She was extremely mad that Smooth stopped her from plan. She planned on throwing eggs at Ciara when she walked the runway. "Fuck you Smooth, you just make sure that you have my money on Monday or else!" Kayla drove off with her middle finger in the air.

I spit on the ground and shook his head as he watched Kayla drive off. London stepped outside to tell him that Ciara was about to walk out any second. Me and Red went back inside and continued to watch the fashion show. London got on the microphone to introduced Ciara.

"Ladies and gentlemen, thank you all for attending Bella's 5th year anniversary fashion show. Today it was a pleasure and an honor to introduce our new line of lingerie and swimwear. Over the years Bella's Boutique has continued to grow in a positive way. From helping out in the committee, to feeding the homeless and having coat drives, there isn't anyone left out. Bella's Boutiques has grown on the map, with four locations here in Chicago, Atlanta, Texas and Arizona. All of this wouldn't be possible without the vision of one person who always had a love for fashion. So without further ado, ladies and gentlemen, I would like to introduce to you the owner of Bella's Boutiques, Ciara Robinson."

Ciara walked out on the runway with Eric Jr. and Kenya. They all were dressed in all white. Everyone clapped and cheered for Ciara, she waved and blew kisses to the crowd. All of her models stepped back on the stage also wearing all white. The photographer snapped a lot of pictures as the pose for him. Ciara looked beautiful in her white, long flowing gown. It was something about seeing white against her dark smooth skin. Eric Jr had on a white suit and a fresh pair of Air Force Ones. Kenya looked very pretty in her white dress. I clapped and cheered my baby on with the crowd. We locked eyes and she winked at me. The music came on and everyone started to socialize and shop. I grabbed the lovely box of one hundred dollar roses and presented it to her in the back.

"You did an awesome job gorgeous, I'm so very proud of you." I gave Ciara a kiss on the cheek, not wanting to mess up her makeup. My son gave me a hug and so did Kenya. The photographer took photos of us. I was also wearing all white, Ciara told me to make sure that I had on my white attire. We all celebrated and sipped champagne as the guest shopped.

As everyone hugged and greeted me, I saw that Alicia was having a rough time with her mom. Alicia mother was being very loud, embarrassing that poor girl. Politely I excused myself and walked over to them. I took pictures with Alicia and her mom and asked to speak with her mom in private. Alicia stayed with her boyfriend Bobby as me and her mom walked off to the side.

"Hello Cathy, I'm very that happy that you could make it. Do you mind keeping your voice down, you're talking a little too loud? Another thing that I want to talk to you about is your drinking problem." Cathy looked at me with a look of shame in her eyes. "Whenever you're ready to get some help it can be arranged. Alicia shared a few things with me about her childhood. Alicia and I have something in common. My mother was addicted to alcohol when I a teenager. She battle with alcoholism on and off over the years. Last month my mother died due to alcoholism."

Cathy started to cry. "I don't want to die and I don't mean to embarrass her." She cried.

"You don't have to cry Cathy. There is help available for you, you can start tomorrow if you like."

"I would love to do that. Thank you Ciara."

"Great tomorrow meet me at my boutique in the afternoon and we can go from there." I gave Cathy a hug. She needed it, you can see it in her eyes that she has been through a lot.

For the remainder of the night I celebrated with my guest. I was so happy that my 5th year anniversary show was such a success. I looked out into the crowd and I could see Jas clapping for me. I smiled at her and whispered I love you. Jas said I love you too sis and disappeared.

Monday morning crept around quickly, just like I needed it to. My lawyer and I sat at the table discussing my options when it came to my parental rights. On my end everything was going fine and working out in my favor. The only person that was holding us was Kayla. She was aware of the court date and knew how important it was for her to be here. Last night I quick paid her half of the money to account. She will receive the other half after she signs the documents. Moments later in strolls Kayla dressed in all black and wearing black shades like she was attending a funeral.

"Good morning, sorry that I'm late." She giggled, taking a seat on the other side of the table.

The judge walked in sitting across the table from us, placing on his glasses. My lawyer presented him with our documents and he went over them. He asked Kayla if she agreed to these terms, she had no problem with them. Ready to get everything over with so that she could receive the rest of her money. With every reply that she gave it was a giggled followed behind it. She signed the paperwork, everything was finalized and in writing. I shook my lawyer hand as Kaylah watched from the sidelines with a smile on her face. She left out ahead of me, waiting by the elevator.

Walking out a happy man, I pushed one button sending her the rest of her funds.

Kayla and I stepped onto the elevator, we were alone. "Thank you for taking my daughter away from me forever. You finally got what you wanted." Kayla replied.

"No Kayla, you finally got what you wanted. I hope that you don't spend that fifty thousand all at once." The elevator opened and I stepped into the lobby, walked out the door and went to get into my car. Never in my life have I ever felt like a weight was lifted off of me. No more Kayla, no more drama and no more bullshit. Variyah can grow up in a better household now with two parents that love her.

I made it to my mother house to tell her the great news. She was so happy that she started praising the God. "Eric you have no idea how hard that I've been praying for this moment. I didn't want my granddaughter growing up like her mother continuing the generational curse. Now son you have to get yourself together and settle down. That would make me a happier mother."

"Mom don't worry, I'm already a step ahead of you." I gave my mother a hug and spent the rest of the day with my daughters Erica and Variyah. When Variyah asked to speak to her mother, I called Kayla for her but she never answered.

Baby my bank account was finally back booming. Now that I had the money, I decided that maybe I should just close my shoe store. With that money and the money that I have saved I will start over. Not knowing what I was going to do, it was best if I went back to scamming and hustling. When I was doing that money was flowing in great. This time I around I wasn't going to have a team and get myself popped off again.

For the last couple days I've been so busy at my shoe store. I threw a big sale to get the people to come in. Also, I upgraded in my marketing and promotion. Things were flowing, Smooth was right, all I had to do was focus on my store. From that moment that was only thing that mattered. I had to get my paper game up if I wanted to continue to be a boss bitch. Over the days Smooth has been calling me and leaving messages. Variyah wanted to talk to me, but I felt too ashamed to even tell my daughter that she would be living with her dad instead of me. Doing what I do best, I fell back only focusing on my paper. After a while I blocked Smooth number all together. I will get back to my baby girl when the time is right.

This silly bitch Kayla got her money and said fuck her daughter. Honestly this is what I really wanted, but I hate to see Variyah crying out for her mother's love and attention. She was a child and didn't deserve it. All of this caused me to spoil Variyah more, never telling her no and allowing her to break a few rules. I even bought her little gifts to make her feel appreciated. My mother noticed what I was doing and demanded that I stop. She warned me that I was raising her the wrong way and if I continue it, Variyah will be a problem when she gets older. Erica was affected by all the things that I was doing. She leashed out a few times, but nothing outrageous. All of this was taking a toll on me. Ciara was the only woman that understood and stepped in. She spent time with girls like she was their mom, while I spent more time with Junior. Slowly we were working out to be a family again. I still haven't told Ciara about the procedure that I went through. No time was ever a good time to talk to her about it. Ciara still had to finalize her divorce and fly back to Arizona to handle things there. After I fucked Kanye up he went on by his business and made things a lot easier on Ciara. He still tries to act tough when he knows that I am around. I told Ciara that I never wanted Kanye around my son again. Kayne has yet to speak or utter my son name out of his mouth, he didn't want me to knock his teeth out his fucking mouth again.

Chapter Eighteen

Time was going by really fast and I still had things that needed to get done. Kanye wasn't really making it easier for me when it came to Kenya. I didn't bother to involve Smooth in that because Kenya wasn't his daughter. Today was the moment when I had to fly back to Arizona to see the divorce lawyer. Kelly opened up her schedule and came with me. I only brought Kenya with me, leaving Eric Jr. with his father. Smooth made it very clear to me not to ever have his son around Kanye again. Respecting his wishes I did that, but I didn't blame him. Kanye had the nerve to ask me if I was staying at the house with him when I arrived to Arizona. I laughed at such a request, I will never sleep with that man again if was the last man on earth. Kelly, Kenya and I stayed got a hotel suite during our stay. Smooth facetime me all night and Ant did the same with Kelly. Our men were crazy, but we loved their crazy asses.

Monday morning rolled around and it was time for court. I don't know why I was nervous, but Kelly had my back. Do you know when we arrived Kanye had another white woman with him. Kelly refrained me from snapping out.

"Remember Ciara you will be divorced soon. Let's get the bullshit over with." Kelly whispered in my ear.

Exhaling, I took a deep breath and a look at the time on my Rolex watch. Where in the hell was the judge at, he was running ten minutes late. Kenya was sitting in the room being watched by a female attendant. Children weren't allowed in divorce court, things could get ugly and some cases can be damaging to them over the years. The way how Kanye rolled in here with another woman today was a prime example of why children shouldn't be in court. Finally the judge came in and we were sworn in. My lawyer presented my case first. Shortly after Kanye's lawyer represented him, tell me why the bastard had the nerve to act like Smooth was a danger to his daughter. He brought up the fight that he provoked and pictures of his injuries. Knowing Kanye so well, I came prepared for this. I had the police report that proved that Kanye started everything, the police asked my mom neighbors who witness everything. Kanye also was locked up and later bailed out of jail. I also printed out the threaten text messages that he sent me. I had copies of Kanye and his mistress in our pool at home. I also had the text messages of him begging me to take him back. The judge dismissed that and took a ten minute break.

"Kelly I pray that this is over with. I'm just ready to get my things and move back to Chicago." I said. Kanye looked over at me with a smirk on my face. I rolled my eyes and continued to talk to Kelly.

"Girl ignore him, you got this." Kelly said.

Twelve minutes later the judge walked back. My heart was racing, please lord don't let this be a continuous. Judge Hartgrove agreed in my favor. I was so happy that I shouted in joy. Kanye had to pay me two thousand a month in child support and for Kenya's schooling and medical expenses. Due to me moving back to Chicago, he was allowed to keep Kenya over the winter and summer break. He also had to pay me twenty five hundred a month in alimony. I rolled my eyes at that because Kanye made damn good money. It was low because I didn't really depend on Kanye and had a successful business. I got the house as well and planned on selling it. Kanye didn't seem mad, he was never good at showing his emotions. He requested to see Kenya, which wasn't a problem. The woman brought Kenya out to the courtroom. She walked in slowly not knowing who to go to.

"Kenya my baby girl, I miss you so much." Kanye said.

Kenya walked up to me and sat in my lap. She looked at her father and the woman that sat next to him. "Hi daddy. Who is that lady by you?" Kenya asked.

"Baby, she's just a friend of your daddy." Kanye said.

Kenya took a minute to warm up to him and was back smiling in his arms. I wasn't the type of woman to keep a child away from their father, but Kanye and I had to have a talk about different women being around my daughter.

"Excuse me Kanye, I'll appreciate it if you not bring a woman around my daughter without running it by me first." I said.

"So now you think that you can tell me who to date?" Kanye said smartly.

"No, I'm not you. I just don't want several women around my daughter. That can confuse a child and I don't need to add any more confusion to her life."

"Ciara I was trying to avoid all the confusion in the first place. You were the one who didn't want to work things out." Kanye dumb ass said.

"You should've thought about that before you started sleeping with other women. Oh but that's water under the bridge now. Like I said, don't have your different women around my child."

Kanye looked at me stupid. His little white girlfriend was beet red and embarrassed. Poor woman didn't know what she was getting herself into. Maybe it was best that Kanye had him a younger woman. Someone that he can control. I didn't want to keep complaining about her being a white woman, but we all know that they only chase after black men for one thing. Kanye loved to have his head pumped up. I guess that I was too much of a successful black woman for him. I walked out of the courtroom one happy woman. Kanye had thirty days to vacant my house.

"Kelly I did it. We have to celebrate sis. Who run the world?" I sang.

"Girls!" Kenya yelled in laughter.

Kelly and I started cracking up laughing at Kenya. She was sitting in her car seat singing and eating chips.

"Ciara we got us a singer in the family." Kelly laughed.

I drove off and headed back to our hotel. I couldn't wait to tell Smooth the good news.

The next day I had the movers ready to go by the house. I had to be ushered by the police while everything was taking place. Kanye had to be present as well, he was wearing a sweat suit and some gym shoes when we arrived. Kenya was at her grandmother Cathy house, she made back up with me and Kenya was asking for her. With Kenya not being around, I could get plenty of things done. The movers were ready to get things started and so was I. I started upstairs in my room closet. Kelly and I packed up my clothes and shoes. The movers were downstairs in the kitchen packing those things.

"You can have it all, I will just start over again." Kanye said to the movers.

"Please don't listen to him, he's just in the way." I told the movers who laughed.

Kanye became livid and tried to act a fool. The police told him that if he couldn't cooperate that he would be removed from the premises. Kanye stopped being a pain in the ass, taking a seat on the couch. He was such an asshole at times. We started at nine am and was finished by four pm. The place was empty except for Kanye things and the household appliances. I didn't bother to take the food, but my petty ass could've have. Kelly and I was so damn tired and needed to rest. Before the moving company pulled off I took pictures of my belongings. They went over the correct address and location to where they were going. Off to Illinois, the movers pulled off and hit the highway.

Kenya was having such a good time with her grandma that Cathy asked to keep her until I left. I didn't have a problem with that, Kenya wasn't going to see her again till winter break. I soaked my bones in the Jacuzzi and sipped on some champagne. Kelly was busy making love on the phone to Ant. I thought about Smooth and the new beginning in my life. Finally Kelly got off the phone and joined me in the Jacuzzi.

"Damn can you please let Ant breath? Every hour you check in with your sprung ass." I laughed as I poured champagne in the flute.

"For your information, I'm in love. Now you on the other hand is sprung on Smooth. You two just need to make it happen." Kelly said.

"You're right, I'm back sprung on him. Kelly I didn't have any intentions on falling back in love with him. I don't know what it is, but I'm afraid sis." I admitted.

"Afraid of what? Real love?" Kelly asked.

"No, not love. I just got a divorce, do you think that I need to have a break before I jump back into another relationship? I just don't want to move too fast." I said.

"Move too fast? Ciara I'm a firm believer of that everything happen for a reason. Maybe you and Kanye failed and you catching him because it was meant for you and Smooth to get back together. How many married women actually catch their cheating spouse without investigating? All I can tell you is to do what you feel is right for you. But, between you and me I heard that Smooth wants to remarry you." Kelly sipped on her champagne looking at me sideways.

Thinking about that last statement, Smooth wanting to remarry me had me speechless. Life is so funny, just the other night I had a dream that I was walking down the aisle getting married, but I didn't see who I was marrying. The scaring thing about my dream was that my mother was there and so was Jas, she was a brides mate. Kelly and I continued to talk and catch up with a lot of things. It was something that we rarely ever get a chance to do. She finally opened up about her mother and going to see her. I'm very proud of her for doing that. In the past Kelly would never talk about her mom and if you asked her a question about her she wouldn't say much. Always feeling like overtime she would come out of that shell. She also shared with me that she wanted to have another baby. That was a whole another situation right there.

"Have you discussed having another baby with Ant?" I asked.

"Yes and he's down for it. We have been having sex all day and night. You know that I was on the depo shot so I'm hoping that I conceive soon." Kelly said.

"Girl I wouldn't know what I would do with another baby right now. Good thing that I don't have to worry about that because Smooth got that taken care of. Besides between him and me we have enough." I said.

"Well I'm thirty so I want to knock one more out the way. Then after that I'm finished, I want another girl" Kelly said.

"Do your thing sis, you know that I'll be here to support you. Another God baby for me Sis! Speaking of children, Denise quads birthday party is next week. I have to get them something soon." I said.

"Red and Denise anniversary is coming up in October too. They are going to Asia and invited all of us. Are you going to be joining us this year?" Kelly asked me smiling.

"Smooth did bring that up. Now that I've wrapped everything up here, yes I am going. I've always wanted to visit Asia." I said.

Kelly was so happy to have me back a part of the gang again. I'm not going to lie, I was happy to be back included. The next day I got both Eric Jr. and Kenya's transfer from their schools. Their principal hated to see them go. Goodbye Arizona, I enjoyed you. Hello again Chicago.

Chapter Nineteen

"Daddy you have to come now. I think that something is wrong with grandma. When I woke up this morning she wasn't up like she normally would be. I went in her room and she was still in bed sleeping, but she's not moving." Erica said.

I jumped out of my bed and threw on some clothes quickly. I didn't like what I was hearing from Erica. "Baby girl where are you right now?" I asked her.

"I'm in grandma's room watching her in bed. Variyah is still asleep in the room and so is Junior." Erica said.

"Okay Erica baby, please call 911. I'm on my way right now." I said.

Vell was sleep in my guest room downstairs. I rushed in the room to wake him up and told him what was going on. He got dressed while I called Erica back and stayed on the phone with her till the paramedics arrived. Vell jumped behind the wheel diving as I tried to remain calm. Erica told me that the paramedics finally arrived and started to check on my mom. She put me on speaker phone so that I could hear what they were doing and saying. All I could hear was a lot of moving around and mumbling voices. Erica was still on the line.

"What are they doing Erica?" I asked her.

"They told me to step out of the room daddy." Erica said.

One of the paramedics started talking to Erica asking her if she was the only one in the home. I spoke up because I could hear them.

"Excuse Mr. I'm her father and on the way there right now. Can you please tell me what's going on with my mom?" I demanded.

"Sir, we suggest that you get here as soon as possible. By law I'm not alone to tell you what's going on over the phone." The paramedic said.

"Fuck!" I was angry. If they weren't taking her to the hospital that only meant one thing.

Vell sped on the expressway, we were now sixteen minutes away. He was going seventy miles per hour punching it. Right about now I didn't give a fuck about the state troopers pulling us over!

When we got there I rushed into my mother's house. Erica, Variyah and Junior was sitting on the couch next to a female police officer. They were happy to see me and I was happy to know that they were ok. I ran upstairs, the moment that I saw her I knew that she was dead. My mother was so full of life that seeing her in bed was not normal. I sat down next to her and kissed her on the cheek. This couldn't be happening to me right now. Not my mother, she was all that I had. I kissed her again on the forehead as I cried. Vell stood back watching me not saying a word. My mother was dead, the only woman that I had in my corner for many years.

It was very hard for me to watch them take my mother's body out of the house in a body bag. The paramedics didn't know what the cause of death was, I had to find that out from the coroner after the autopsy was performed. My daughters were crying taking it extremely hard. Erica was shaking so bad that she was scaring me. Vell took the time to call everyone and tell them what happened.

As we boarded our early morning flight, I received a phone call from Vell. Immediately my heart started to race when I saw his name pop up on my phone screen. Vell was staying with Smooth while he was in Chicago. The only reason why he would be calling me is because Smooth was in position to. All kinds of thoughts flashed in my head. You never know with all the bullshit that goes down in Chicago what could've occurred. Bracing myself for good news I answer the phone.

"Hey Vell what's up?" I answered.

"Ciara where are you know?" Vell asked, making me worried.

"Me, Kelly and Kenya just got on our flight to Chicago. Why, what's going on is Smooth okay?"

"Smooth is okay, but his mom just passed away." Vell said.

"What are you serious?!" I yelled causing everyone on the plane to look at me like I was crazy. For a second I forgot where I was at. Kelly asked me what was going on, but I had to see how Smooth was doing.

"Where is Smooth?! Okay I will call you when we land in Chicago." I hung up the phone and turned to look at Kelly.

"Ciara what happened? What is Vell talking about?" Kelly asked.

"Smooth mother just died." I told Kelly.

"No way, not sweet Ms. Jackson. I know that Smooth is taking it very hard." Kelly said as she pulled out her cell phone to call Ant. Ant was with Smooth and everyone else at the house.

This three hour flight was going to be the longest ever.

My cell phone woke up as it blared loudly. Not knowing who it was I answered the phone. "Hello, who is this?" I was knocked the hell out.

"Say that again. Smooth mother died? Wait I'm still sleep, I'm getting up right now."

It was Aaliyah that just called me saying that Ms. Jackson was dead. She said that Vell had called and told her. As I rolled over to see the stranger that was lying in the bed with me, all I could think about was the comment that I made about her being old. Knowing Smooth I know that he was going crazy right now. I know how it feels to lose your mother. To this day I still have nightmares of the time when my mother committed suicide after she killed my grandfather. Since I've blocked Smooth's number, I haven't heard from him or my daughter. Now I had no choice but to be there for Variyah and face Smooth. It's been three weeks since I've heard from him. Over the last three weeks things have been going pretty good in the money department. Going back to my scammer ways, I was making three hundred a day. It wasn't much, but it was a good start. My shoe store wasn't even bringing in that kind of money. The stranger in my bed starting moving around. I took a good look at him, he was dark skinned, with a head full of dreads and body made of muscles. His dick was brick hard, standing at attention. My pussy was wet and ready, morning sex was a great way to start the day.

One hour later the stranger was in the shower, I was trying to remember his name. He took his clothing in the bathroom with him, I had no wallet to go through to find out his name. He stepped out of my bathroom fully dressed, smoking a blunt.

"See you around beautiful." He kissed me on the forehead. I hit his blunt a few times before he left and told him to call me. He promised to call me, but I knew that he was lying. I told him to lock my door on the way out behind him. My nose was itching, so I took a line of coke to ease my urge. I took a look at my daughter and Smooth's picture in the broken picture frame that sat on my dresser. Suddenly Smooth came alive from the picture and starting walking toward me saying awful things. Variyah starting crying out for me, telling me that I was a bad mother.

"Get away from me! Get out my house now!" I screamed, knocking everything off of my dresser. Their faces disappeared and the voices went away.

Ant was waiting to pick us up at the airport. We all sat in the car quietly on our way home. I still haven't spoken to Smooth about everything that was going on. I was worried and concerned about him.

"Where is Smooth and the children? I asked Ant.

"Everyone is at his mom house. Smooth is hurting really bad, not saying too much of a word. I'm going to pick up some wings and fish from JJ's before we head back. It's been a very long day for us all." Ant said.

He stopped to pick up some food and continued on to Smooth's mother house. The whole clique was there I see, from all the cars that was parked out front. Kenya and I went inside, while Ant and Kelly sat in the truck to talk alone. Everyone gave me a hug and was happy to see me. I looked around for my son and the girls. They were upstairs in their room, I can hear them over my head running around. I went upstairs along with Kenya to check on the kids.

"Mommy, Kenya, you're back." Eric Jr. ran up to me to give me a hug and so did Erica and Variyah.

"How are you guys doing?" I asked as I kissed them on all on the forehead.

"We're okay, but grandma is dead. Daddy says that she is in a better place now." Erica said.

I stared at Erica and could see the pain in her eyes. "Are you hungry? Uncle Ant brought some chicken and fish back. Go downstairs so Kelly can make you a plate." All four of them ran downstairs to eat.

I walked down the hall to Ms. Jackson room where Smooth was. He was sitting alone in his mom chair with her picture in his hand. "Baby I'm here now for you." I gave him a hug.

"Ciara it hurts so bad, she's gone just like that." Smooth said.

"Did they tell you what the cause of death was?"

"Not yet, I will find out tomorrow. Damn! I hate that I wasn't here to anything, maybe if I was she would still be alive." Smooth said.

"Smooth you can't beat yourself up for not being here. Everything will be okay, Ms. Jackson was tired babe. When I was here she shared with me how she was tired of taking all that medication and was always in pain."

"She would've been eighty in December. I had a lot of plans for her. I loved that woman so much." Smooth said.

"She loved you too Smooth. At times I wished that I had that same time of love from my mom." I admitted.

Smooth and I hugged one another and cried. After a while I got him to cheer up a bit. He was going through his family photos, I laughed at Smooth's baby pictures. He looked like his mother so much. When we ran across a picture of his father, Smooth didn't say a word. I didn't want to pressure him about his father. He rarely talked about him, all I know is that he went away leaving his mother to raise him alone. After three hours of being upstairs, I suggested that we go down with our friends.

"Smooth everyone would like to see you now. Are you fine to go downstairs now?' I asked him.

"Yeah, I'm straight now." Smooth left his mother picture on her pillowcase. I turned off the light and closed the door behind us.

We went downstairs to join everyone who was patiently to see Smooth. They all gave their condolences and sympathy. By night time I was back in Smooth's arms, right by his side.

Chapter Twenty

Ms. Jackson funeral ceremony was today. Smooth was taking it better than he was before. Her ceremony was lovely, it didn't seem like a funeral. It felt more like a celebration, she was deeply loved by many. Smooth looked so damn fine dressed in his all black suit. I had to contain myself, but tonight it was going down. Everyone was dressed in all black, even the children. During the ceremony Erica, Eric Jr. and Variyah all said a poem that I helped them write, about their grandmother. It was so sweet of them and had everyone in tears. The preacher had to cut it down to two minutes for everyone that had something to say. Everything was going fine until the devil walked into the church. Kayla was wearing a pair of shades, with long black weave down hair back and wearing a red mini dress. She was dressed unappropriated for a funeral.

"Typical Kayla, never turning her hoe down." Kelly whispered in my ear.

"She so damn thirsty for attention. As long as she stay out of my way we cool. I still owe her a beat down." I whispered back to Kelly.

"Girl you know how I get down. I don't care where we are. I'll still tag that ass." Kelly smiled.

"I know crazy, that's why you're my bestie." I said.

At that moment I reminisced about the time when Kelly and Jasmine help me fight those hood rats when we were in the group home. Kelly is my day one, since a one. I know how bad she wants to fight Kayla, but Kayla would never pull it with her. When it was time for everyone to view Ms. Jackson body. Kayla switched up to her casket and gave her a kiss on the cheek. I wanted to throw up, she was so damn fake. Kelly and I shook our heads at that phony hoe.

After the funeral Kayla walked over to her daughter. Variyah was happy to see her mom. Smooth was on the other side of the room with some of his family members. When Kayla bent over she bumped me on purpose. I let it slide because of where we were, besides I didn't want to embarrass her in front of her daughter. Kelly on the other hand didn't care.

"Excuse you, damn please go over there somewhere. You too close and liable to get smacked by me. You know that don't nobody rock with you over here." Kelly said,

Kayla looked at Kelly and rolled her eyes. "Come have a seat over here with mommy Variyah." Kayla walked away and took a seat at another table.

"Stupid bitch, I'm ready to slap the taste out of her mouth." Kelly said.

"Kelly just ignore her, all she wants in attention." I said.

"Yes you're right about that. Take a look at what I see." Kelly pointed at something.

I turned around to see Kayla on the side of Smooth with Variyah snapping pictures. Smooth looked upset, but played along. He picked Variyah up and continued to talk to his great aunt. Kayla got on to Smooth not paying her any attention and walked out of the hall. I got up to be by Smooth's side. Normally I wouldn't be all up under Smooth, but I see that I had to make my presence known with Kayla around. She was trying her best to be irrelevant. Now was not the time for all the bullshit that Kayla was pulling at Smooth's mother repast. For her to be older than me she was so damn childish. His family members were happy to see Smooth and I back together. Although it was a sad moment right now. We all took several pictures with his family members. You know black people only get together on three occasions, family reunions, weddings and funerals. Many of his family members were in town from down south. Smooth haven't seen a lot of his cousins since he was little. Tommy and Tia was there as well, they arrived late.

"I'm sorry that we're late everyone. It was a flight delay because of a computer clinch with American Airlines. We had to book a flight with Southwest to get here and fly into Midway." Tia said.

"Yes I heard about that on the news. I'm so happy that you two made it safely." I gave Tia and Tommy a hug.

Tommy went to go holler at Smooth and the rest of their family members. Me, Tia, Kelly and Denise were standing off to the side. Tia pulled us to the table to have a seat. "Why is Krazy Kayla standing outside puffing on a cigarette dressed like a hooker?" Tia asked.

"Oh she's still here? We all thought that she left forty minutes ago." Kelly said.

"Her thirsty ass trying to get Smooth's attention, but it isn't working." I said.

"Oh that's why she dressed like a two dollar whore." Tia laughed.

"I don't even know why she is here anyway. I thought that she didn't care for Ms. Jackson." Denise said.

"That's true and I know for sure that Ms. Jackson wasn't too fond of her either. It's all a front, she hasn't talked to Variyah's in three weeks. Smooth said that he has been trying to get in touch with her, but she blocked his calls. Then she's going to roll in here like she family. I'm tired of that bitch. I'm more upset about how she is treating her damn daughter like she doesn't exist. It's not acceptable to pop in and out of a child's life."

"She certainly is too old to be acting like she's young. Kayla is thirty five years old and knows better." Kelly made a valid point.

Usually I wouldn't allow her to get under my skin, but when I heard that she was still outside I was pissed off. Kayla had no business being here in the first fucking place. The only person that's getting hurt out of all this is Variyah. She will do better by just not coming around period. I didn't want to tell them that Smooth paid her money just to cooperate. It's like she just come around to start shit, like when she showed up to my fashion show uninvited.

The repast was over with and we all gathered to leave. I was happy to see Smooth back laughing again. The children were with Smooth and I as we walked to his truck. It was seven pm and still daylight outside. Out of nowhere Kayla ran up on me, punching me in my face. At first I didn't know who hit me until I heard Variyah say her mother name. I grabbed Kayla by her long weave and slung her on the ground. I stomped her in the stomach, trying to stomp the air out of her. Kayla started yelling for Smooth to help her.

"Don't call on Smooth hoe, he don't fuck with you!" **PUNCH! PUNCH! PUNCH!**

Smooth stopped me, "Chill baby before you kill her." He walked me off. "You thirsty bitch!" I yelled snatching the water bottle out of Denise hands and throwing the water on her. Ant was driving down the street when it all went down. Kayla ran off in front of his truck barely hitting her. Kelly jumped out of the truck and started fighting Kayla. Kayla was so afraid of Kelly that she didn't fight her back. Ant pulled Kelly away, while one of Smooth's family members helped Kayla to her car. Everyone watched as she got her ass beat twice. She was fighting me like she was high off something. Smooth, the children and I went back to his mother house. I apologized to them because they didn't deserve to see all of that. Children repeat what they see and hear. I pray that they don't ever think that fighting is always acceptable.

Smooth ain't shit for letting them jump on me. That little bitch Kelly always interfering in Ciara bullshit. This was not over between the both of us. I'm going to catch up with Kelly ass up at her real estate company. Ciara was getting hers too on Monday when she open up her boutique. Everyone was blowing up my phone. I didn't bother to answer because all they wanted to talk about was the fight. I rushed home to clean myself up. Ciara had managed to fuck my face up, but it wasn't stopping shit. I soaked in the tub, my body was sore as fuck. All I wanted right now was a massage and some dick. I called my sex buddy, the stranger who was in my bed a few days ago. He said that he would be by when his woman went to work tonight. In the meantime I needed some coke to calm my nerves. I made a phone call and had my supplier to drop me some off. A quarter after ten he showed up with my shit, I paid him and he went on his way. Line after line I sniffed it up my nose. The pain was beginning to go away, making my pussy wetter. I started to get hot so I stripped down to my underwear and turned the music on. My sex buddy arrived right on time. He undressed and rolled up his blunt while I did my coke. I added coke to the blunt so it could be powerful. We were high than a mother fucker and started fucking like rabbits. He didn't even wear a condom, he just slid in me raw. I didn't care because raw sex was the best sex. He entered every hole in my body. He was freaky, I loved a freak. As he fucked me all I seen was Smooth face.

"Oh yes fuck me! Fuck me harder Smooth!" I yelled. He didn't care who name I was calling him, as long as he got his nut off.

It was six am in the morning, the stranger had to go home before his woman discovered that he wasn't there. He shook Kayla, but she didn't move. Her head limped to the right side with slob running down her mouth. The stranger smacked and shook her, but she didn't respond. He checked her pulse, she didn't have one. He got dressed quickly and got the fuck out of there, leaving Kayla's dead body in bed. He felt bad for leaving her that way, but he couldn't go back to prison he was on his second strike. He went home, took a shower and went to sleep as if nothing happened.

When his woman came home from work he kissed her and fucked her raw the same way that he just fucked Kayla.

Chapter Twenty One

Last night Smooth and I made love after we put the children to sleep. I can't believe that Smooth and I actually made love in his mother house. I felt free when I had sex with him this time because I was no longer attached to Kanye. I woke up in the morning cooking breakfast while everyone was sleep. The smell of the food woke them up one by one. It's been such a very long time since I've cooked a big meal like this. For Erica, Variyah and Kenya to be little girls, they had a big appetite. I cooked turkey patties, links, pancakes and eggs. We all sat at the table eating breakfast like one big happy family. Despite yesterday life was pretty good. That dirty bitch Kayla made me break my damn nail, but I was fine. After we finished eating, the children went back to their rooms. It was Sunday, chill day so Smooth let them have some fun amongst themselves.

Smooth and took a shower and had some fun. For the first time we were both enjoying one another. It was like it was meant to be this way. We got out of the shower soaking wet.

"You wrong for making me get my hair wet Smooth." I hit him with a pillow.

"That weave will dry off, what you wearing Brazilian?" Smooth laughed.

"You play too much." I brushed my hair with my paddled brush. I watched Smooth in the mirror, he was getting something from under the mattress. I put my hair up in a ponytail and took seat on the edge of the bed. Smooth pulled out a ring box and dropped down on his knee.

"No way." I cried into my hands, covering up my face.

"Yes you know how long that I've been waiting to make you my wife again. The first time we didn't get a chance to grow together. Now that I have you back in my life again, I'm not letting you get away. Ciara we both been through a lot, some good and bad, but you never left my side. You're my soul mate. I love you Blackbone, would you marry me?" Smooth cried.

"Yes I will." I cried as he opened the box. It was a seven carat, emerald cut diamond ring. "Oh my God it's beautiful Smooth." He slid the ring on my finger.

Smooth smiled, "Thank Kelly for picking out the ring.

I kissed him and cried. "You better keep me this time and never let me go."

"Ciara we all we got. You have no idea how many times that I wanted to fly to Arizona to kidnap you and my son. It feels good to have you back in my life. I want another child with you, I want expand our family." Smooth said.

I looked confused. "How do you expect to do that? Didn't you have a vasectomy?" I asked him.

"Yes I did, but last month I had it reversed. That's how serious I am about everything that I've said."

"Eric are you serious? I didn't know that they could do that? I mean, I wouldn't expect you to do that. Wow." You know that I was shocked when I called him by his first name. I paused for a second, Smooth looked concerned. "I wouldn't mind having another boy around." I smiled and said.

Smooth smiled and kissed my belly. "Tonight let's continue to work on making our baby boy."

I laughed as he kissed my belly. Moments later Smooth's cellphone rang. He answered to see what Ant wanted. "Say what?" Smooth turned on the television to ABC News.

It was breaking news story about a woman being found dead in her home located in LaGrange. Smooth and I sat back listening to the news reporter. He got dressed quickly and told Ant to meet him at the police station.

"What's going on Smooth? Do you know the woman who they're talking about?" I asked him.

"Baby I'll explain everything when I get back." Smooth kissed me on the forehead. "I'll call you in an hour, I love you." Smooth ran down the stairs and out the door.

I was clueless to everything that was going on. Before I tried to do my research, I went to check on the children. Erica and Junior were playing the game. Variyah and Kenya were watching a Barbie movie on their tablet. Okay they were cool and behaving. Now I had to get on top of what the hell was going on with Smooth and Ant.

I called Kelly, she answered on the first ring. "Girl I was just about to call you. Rumor has it, Kayla was found died in her home. They say that she may have committed suicide, but I don't know yet. Ant and Smooth is going up to the police station to find out what's going on." Kelly said.

"Damn! I know that I didn't like her, but I don't wish death on nobody. When Ant called, Smooth answered and turned on the news. I had no idea what was going on because I never knew where the hell she lived." I said.

"I feel sorry for Variyah." Kelly said.

"Yes, I do to. I'm going to let Smooth handle this one. I dealt with the death of Rochelle and had to explain it to Erica. I don't think that I can do this all over again." I said.

"Smooth got a thang for crazy bitches. You better not go out like them friend." Kelly laughed.

She was always turning a bad situation into something good. "Trust me, I'm not about that crazy life. I got children to raise and moves to make. Anyway, thank you for picking out my ring sis. I love it." I changed the subject.

"Oh! He proposed?! You're welcome, I picked it out the week before we went to Arizona. It was so hard to tell you." Kelly laughed. "It almost slipped out a few times, but Smooth made me promise not to say anything."

"Did you know that he reversed his vasectomy, since everyone keeping secrets?" I asked her.

"Wait? Hold up wait?! Are you serious Ciara?" Kelly asked me, she was shocked just like me. "You need to ask to see some proof. I'm sure that he has some paperwork or to prove it."

"Oh yes, I don't have a problem with asking him. He told me that he wanted to have another baby."

"Did you tell him what you told me while we were in Arizona?" Kelly asked me.

"Actually I have a change of heart about having another child. I told him that I would love to have his son. We were in the middle of celebrating until Ant called."

"Sis we should get pregnant together. Let's do it, so our babies can grow up together."

"That's what it's looking like because Smooth and I have been fucking nonstop. All day, all night and he haven't been pulling out, because I knew that he couldn't have anymore. Hell I might be pregnant now." I laughed.

"It will happen when we both not concentrating on it. Well I'm about to go visit my mom right now. Your god children are bugging me, they're ready to go." Kelly said.

"Tell Jasmine and Justin that they better be nice. Tell your mother that I said hello and talk to you later." I said.

"Okay I'll call you when I get back in tonight. Love you Sis." Kelly said.

"Love you too." Click!

Damn another crazy bitch bites the dust. I know that was mean to think, but I was getting tired of that crazy bitch Kayla. Ever since I've been back in town the bitch has been at my neck. The old me would've killed the bitch myself. The new me didn't have time to be fighting out here in the streets like I'm young. Over the last five years I've grown into mature woman. I have no control over death, I just pray that it done in my circle. You know what they say, death normally comes in three's. Hopefully the grim reaper has moved on. This summer I never intended on burying my mother or getting a divorce. I had so many great plans with my ex-husband and children that I was excited about. We plan, God laughs. I just pray that God covers Eric, me and the children. I love them all so much. I got down on my knees to pray.

"Oh Lord, grant me the grace to love you more and more each day. May my family learn what it means to love you with all our hearts, souls and strength. Help my fiancée and

I to be diligent teachers and doers of the Word in our home, when we sit at home, when we are driving around town and when we go to sleep at night. May your Word, your love and your sacrifice ever be on the forefront of our minds and hearts. Only by your grace and for your glory. Amen."

Smooth walked through the door around four pm. The children and I were in the kitchen preparing dinner. They were such a big help, plus it kept them from driving me crazy. "Hey hubby how was your day?" I asked him as I washed my hands.

Smooth walked me over to the couch, we both took a seat. "I know that you heard that the woman that they found dead in her apartment was Kayla. She died of a drug overdose." He said.

"Drug overdose? What type of drugs was she on?" I asked.

"Kayla had a bad coke habit, that's why I fought to have custody of my child. Now I have to break the bad news to Variyah." Smooth said.

"Don't worry, we can do it together. Tonight over dinner we can talk to her about it." I decided not to be petty and leave him hanging, breaking the news by himself.

Smooth went upstairs to take a shower. I stayed in the kitchen cooking pot roast, macaroni and cheese, cabbage and cornbread. We all watched a movie in the front room until dinner was finished. Smooth came downstairs to join us. I almost burned my cornbread dealing with the children. It was time to eat dinner, Smooth sat at the head of the table. For the first time he said the prayer instead of me. My heart raced when it was time to tell Variyah about her mother. Smooth spoke first, I jumped in periodically. Variyah cried when she realized that her mom was dead and never coming back. Smooth and I got up to console her as she cried in our arms.

The children were sleep in their beds. Now it was time for Smooth and I to discuss what we planned to do about our living arrangements. We now each had three properties to maintain. After talking for an hour we both came up with a decision. Smooth was going to sale his home and I was going to rent my mother's house out. We were going to move into his mother house, because her home was the biggest. The area also had the best schooling as well. It all made sense to just have one property to maintain. I opened up more on how I felt about starting all over. Smooth had to understand also that I have four successful Bella Boutiques and that I will have to travel to and from them. I also wanted to open up another location in California and here in Chicago. We also needed to set up a time when we can sit the children down and discuss all of this sudden change. Even though they were children they opinion still matters, more importantly we care how they feel. Smooth new business was due to break ground in the fall. He was excited about all of that. With the life insurance policy that I received on my mother and the settlement I was financially stable for another six years. Smooth also had insurance on his mother as well. The autopsy showed that she died of old age, she was tired and may she continue to rest in peace. Since Kayla didn't have any close family, Smooth was going to have her cremated and give her ashes to Variyah. We both reminisced on the times when we were struggling. Smooth finally opened up and talked about his father. He shared some good and bad moments about him. I trusted Smooth with my secrets and he trusted me with his. It was good that we finally had a chance to talk and communicate. We made a promise to never keep secrets from one another. With Smooth I felt loved and safe. It was a special kind of feeling that he had on my heart. A feeling that never went away, I was just waiting on him to get his act together. Smooth apologized about hurting me in the past with his foolish antics. I forgave him and we put the past behind us. Smooth has finally grown up and owned up to his faults, that's the difference between a man and a boy.

Chapter Twenty Two

I rolled over to an empty spot in my bed, where the hell was Ant? Looking over at the time on the wall, it was eleven am. I sat up, I was feeling light headed. Ant walked into the room, "You finally woke up I see."

"Why did you let me sleep that long?" I asked him.

"I tried to wake you up several times, but you wouldn't wake up. Are you okay baby?"

I tried to stand up. "I feel lightheaded." **Bloop!** I fainted, falling on the floor.

"Kelly! Mom call 911, Kelly just fainted." Ant yelled.

I woke up in the emergency room with my family by my side. They all were happy that I opened my eyes.

"Momma the doctor said that you fainted." Jasmine said.

"Baby you scared us all for a second, but the doctor said that you were fine." Ant kissed me on the forehead.

Marilyn went to go get the doctor and they both walked in. "Hello Kelly, I'm Dr. Johnson your family brought you in for syncope." He said.

"Dr. Johnson I've been very tired lately. I've never fainting before in my life. Can you explained to me why I fainted?" I asked.

"Good question, I'm glad that the family is all here. I ran a few test on you and I have some news. You're pregnant." Dr. Johnson happily said.

"Really?! Ant baby we're pregnant!" I started crying tears of joy.

Ant kissed me on the belly. "My baby having another baby!" he was so happy.

Jasmine and Justin weren't too happy, they were looking sad with their lips poked out. "We don't want a baby sister or brother." They whined.

"Ohhhh, don't tell me that you two are jealous. Your father and I will never stop loving you. It will be cool to have a baby sister or brother to teach new things to." Ant and I gave them both a hug.

Ant couldn't wait to get on the phone to tell Smooth, Red and Vell. "Yeah man I'm having another baby. Kelly is pregnant, for sure party over my house tonight." He laughed as he talked on the phone.

Wow I can't believe that I'm actually having another baby. Thank you God, after this one I'm getting my tubes tied.

The Next Following Weekend

Today Shawn and I went to go visit my mother. This was our first visit that went together, my mother was so happy to see us. She showed us off to her inmate friends like we were little children. I smiled and said hello to them all, not wanting to be mean.

"You're glowing Kelly. If I didn't know any better, I think that you could be pregnant." My mother said.

Shawn and I laughed. "Why are you two laughing at me?" My mother was starting to get upset.

"Calm down momma, you're right Kelly is pregnant." Shawn said.

"Congratulations Kelly! My daughter is having another baby everyone!" My mother had to tell everybody in the visitor room.

"Thank you momma, Anthony and I are so happy. Enough about me, how do you feel about next week?" I asked my mom.

"I feel very excited. I pray to God that these people let me out." My mom said.

"You're going to okay, I spoke to your lawyer. He says that you have a good chance at getting out. No matter what happens we love you very much." Shawn said.

"I'm claiming it! It's time that I come home to my family." My mom started to cry. We told her that everything was going to just fine and not to worry. God got this!

Meanwhile

My pregnancy had me sick as a dog. Morning sickness is the devil. Ant was there to hold my weave every time that I threw up. It had gotten so bad that I had to keep a garbage bag near my bed. By me not keeping any food down caused me to lose a significant amount of weight. I was hospitalized for dehydration, but overall the baby was doing fine. When I was pregnant with Jasmine and Justin I never got sick. This little devil spun that I was carrying was giving me the flux.

I had to work from home, which Ant loved by the way. No matter what I still had houses to sell and money to make. Plus I was still fighting my case against the government, who was trying to get me to settle for little money. Ant new business venture was taking off soon, we both were very excited about that. Marilyn was doing better at being a grandma, stepping her grandma game up. Whenever the baby had me down, she was there to pick up the slack. Ciara surprised me and came by.

"What's up sis? You look so pretty, I brought you some soup, plenty of crackers and apple juice. I hope that it helps with morning sickness." Ciara said.

'Thank you, can you please make me some now. I'm starving, I can't hold anything down. What brings you here?" I asked Ciara.

She was busy at the stove heating me up some soup. "Well I'm here to check on you and to discuss my wedding. Smooth and I are thinking of doing something small and out of the country. We would like to get married in January in Turks & Caicos. I would like for you, Denise, Tia and Aaliyah to be my bride mates. I'm looking to book a family resort, if you don't mind I would like Marilyn to come as well to watch the children when it's adult time. How do you like this idea?" Ciara asked me.

"I love it and down for whatever. Just put me in a pretty gown that shows off my pregnancy." I said.

"Yes, I think that it's best. Besides, both of our parents are deceased, we only have you guys as close family. I was thinking that I want you all to wear lilac. Right now I have to pick out a wedding dress." Ciara went into her duffle bag and pulled out a stack of wedding magazines.

From the look on her face, I can see that this was going to be some work.

Appeal Day

My mother showed up to her appeal dressed in a ladies pant suit that I got her from Lord& Taylor's. She looked very beautiful in it. If I could've gotten her hair done I would've, but her hair looked fine brushed to the back in a bun. My brother, Ant and I were present. She smiled when she saw us all here. My mom and her lawyer sat at the table along with the other respondent. The four people who sat across my mother was going to make the decision on rather or not my mom becomes a free woman. They started right away, I was nervous like I was on trial. Both of the parties presented paperwork while my mother sat there quietly. Finally it was time for my mom to speak.

"I have admitted my guilt and been sentenced to twenty years in prison. However, I do not feel that this punishment is making full penance for my crime. The justice system has made sure that I have been punished, but I want you to understand that I know now how wrong what I did was. Even though there is no justification for my actions, I was blinded by love. If I could take it back, I would. Instead, please know that I will always be haunted by what I did." My mother was sincere with her apology. She took a seat and then look back at us.

I gave her the thumbs up, winked and smiled. The four people on the panel spoke. They talked all that mumbo jumbo, the only thing that I heard was.

"Appeal Granted!"

"Thank you God!" We were all happy and excited, my mother was coming home. Next stop Fox Valley Transition Center in Aurora. After that, home sweet home.

New Beginnings

Today I was starting a new chapter in my life with all my love ones present. Smooth and I were getting married on a beautiful white sanded beach. Shawn has always been a brother figure to me, so he did the honor of walking me down the aisle. I was keeping the tears from falling, because I didn't want to mess up my beautiful make up. Everyone was smiling, my bride mates all looked beautiful in their lilac bride mate gowns. All the children were dressed in all white looking adorable. Smooth looked so fine in his white tuxedo, with his crew by his side. He was crying as I walked down the aisle. I looked into his eyes and smiled. Smooth reached for me but the preacher stopped him.

"Wait young man, I know that she looks good. You will have plenty of time to touch her after I marry you." Everyone laughed. "Now I will start."

"We are gathered here today to witness and to celebrate the joining together of Ciara and Eric in the holy estate of marriage. More than a ceremony, this is the most significant moment of human celebration and personal commitment and should not be entered into lightly, but in the freedom of joy and sober responsibility. Today you will receive God's greatest gift; another person to share life's blessings with, care for, learn with, trust in, change with and to discover the greatness of God's glory."

"Who brings this woman forward to be with this man?" Shawn said I do. "Thank you, please be seated."

"Do you, Groom, solemnly declare in the presence of God and these witnesses that you take this woman, Bride, to be your lawfully wedded wife? Will you love her, comfort her, honor her, keep her in sickness and in health, and cherish forever?"

"I do." Smooth said smiling.

"Do you, Bride, solemnly declare in the presence of God and these witnesses that you take this man, Groom, to be your lawfully wedded husband? Will you love him, comfort him, honor him, keep him in sickness and in health, and cherish forever?"

"I do." I cried and said.

"These wedding rings have neither a beginning nor an end. They are a symbol of everlasting faith and love. May they ever remind you of the solemn vows and obligations that you have this day taken, and keep steadfast therein until the end." Smooth placed the ring on my finger.

"As a sign of my love and my knowledge, that in marrying you, I am becoming much more than I am. I give you this ring with the promise that I will love you and keep my heart open to you all the days of my life." I placed the ring on Smooth's finger.

We both read our vows to one another making everyone cry. They were both short and sweet.

Smooth looked into my eyes. "You have been my best friend, mentor, playmate, confident and my greatest challenge. But most importantly, you are the love of my life and you make me happier than I could ever imagine and more loved than I ever thought possible. You have made me a better person, as our love for one another is reflected in the way I live my life. So I am truly blessed to be a part of your life, which as of today becomes our life together."

I looked into Smooth's eyes. "You are my lover and my teacher. You are my model and my accomplice. And you are my true counterpart. I will love you, hold you and honor you. I will respect you, encourage you and cherish you, in health and sickness, through sorrow and success. For all the days of my life."

"Bride and Groom, you have expressed your love to one another through this commitment and promises you have just made. It is with these in mind that I pronounce you husband and wife. Those whom God hath joined together, let no one put asunder. You may now kiss the bride."

Smooth and I kissed for a very long time. "Get a room!" Ant yelled, laughing at us.

After that we enjoyed the rest of the resort and had a blast. For the first time in such a very long time I was enjoying life again. Smooth and the fellas popped bottles. Too bad that I couldn't drink because I was expecting. Shhh, that was our secret, I planned on telling the rest of them when we get back home. As for Kelly she was having a baby boy. Looks like her wish came true after all, having our children grow up together. I pray to God that it's a boy!

Ciara & Smooth

Forever

The End!

Made in the USA
Lexington, KY
27 September 2018